Rosie's Gold

Can we heal from trauma?

a novel

Nancy Hicks Marshall

Bridgewood Press
Phoenix, Arizona

This is a work of fiction. Any resemblance to persons living or dead is purely coincidental. Any reference to Navajo tradition or the ceremonial sweat lodge experience, while intended to honor and respect the spirit of such ceremonies, was written with the characters and place of this specific work of fiction in mind. Any errors are the responsibility of the author.

I would like to express my appreciation to the following individuals for their varied contributions: Craig Bush, Dan Everly, and Curtis Walker for their knowledge of matters military, PTSD, and ammo reloading; Steve and Marilee Orcutt for information about medicinal remedies; Randall Palmer with answers about equipment and machinery; Kristy Theilen for her insight into farming; Sharon Sarver for her encouragement; Carolyn Brown and Fran Reich for their attention to detail; Polly Kmetz, for helpful insights on yoga practice; Michel and Donnalee Sarda, for their careful editing and invaluable direction; Margy Tays, who understood what Rosie needed; and, especially, my husband Vance, and my children, Elias and Hilary, for allowing me the time and space to follow my leading on Rosie.

NHM

Book design by Bridgewood Press

Library of Congress Cataloging-in-Publication Data

Marshall, Nancy Hicks, 1941-
     Rosie's Gold: can we heal from trauma / by Nancy Hicks Marshall
          p. cm
     ISBN   978-0-927015-42-4 (trade pbk.)
1. Sexual abuse victims—fiction. 2. Young women—fiction. 3.Self-actualization (Psychology) in women—fiction. I. Title
     PS3613.A77426R67 2010
     813".6—dc22
                    2010037910

Printed in the United States of America

In memory of
Gordon Dana Hicks, 1938-1991
Captain, United States Marine Corps
Served in Vietnam 1962-1963

Chapter 1

The drums started beating softly, steadily, like little patters of rain on pine needles. Ten men — a few West Africans, but mostly Americans, each with his own drum — stood like elders, forming a crescent-shaped half-circle in the large gymnasium where Josuf Mbwana, a renowned dance instructor from West Africa, would soon give the signal to start.

Rosie walked barefoot to the back of the gym. Petite, dressed in a black cap-sleeved leotard and multicolored skirt, she moved swiftly, aware that the dance was about to begin. Her blue eyes and delicate pale cheekbones were framed by a full set of dark, shoulder-length curls pressed away from her face under a bandana torn from the hem of her skirt. She felt self-conscious in the gymnasium, despite the subdued lighting, despite the large congregation of mostly hippy-looking white girls in vibrant African colors, many elbowing (so to speak) to be noticed. She in no way stood out among them.

Several mature Black women were also in the crowd of dancers. They tended to be more robust and, as Rosie would soon see, they were more familiar with the dance. She gazed toward the front of the room for Josuf's cue. She saw Hotchkiss, her brother's friend from Flagstaff, standing at a drum.

She thought she'd give a short wave. She looked toward him.

Instead, a tall, older white man to his left caught her eye. He was thin, swarthy, unshaven, with dark eyes and black messy hair. A Jimi Hendrix T-shirt showed years of wear. The jeans were rumpled, though by wear, not design. There was something familiar, unsettling, about his pose as he hovered over his drum. Too familiar, though she was sure he was a stranger. The lanky torso suggested some substance abuse that, even from this distance and with no facts, repulsed her. Yet there was a kind of pucker of the lips, a loosening of the shoulders before playing, that drew her attention. Suddenly she realized that he was looking directly at her. No, he was looking through her. She quickly looked away.

Josuf started with a short introduction and asked the assembled members to first set their minds to the spirit of African dance. "We are bringing ourselves, our bodies, our spirits, close to the Mother Earth and her healing powers, her powers of regeneration. We dance and drum without shoes, to feel her power. If we feel locked in the cage of life, we can now unlock this cage and begin to feel the fullness of our freedom. This is a time to liberate ourselves from fears and inhibitions, to enjoy our sensuous lively beings. We are free, and at the same time we are safe. We work as a community, men and women together, drummers and dancers, tapping into the powers nature has given to us. Let us begin by lightly warming up in a slow dance." He signaled to the drummers.

Rosie had attended a number of dance gatherings. Sometimes it was in classes, throughout Arizona, whenever and wherever they were available. Sometimes drum circles popped up in a plaza in the summer and dancers would enter the round open space that invited color and movement. The drummers would always make room for dancers to enter and then flank them, as if surrounding an altar.

To Rosie, African dance had assumed the place of a virtual altar in her fight against fear. The steadiness of the drums, the unison of the dancers, the leadership of a man like Josuf

— all provided a time and space in which she could express her sensuality and feel entirely safe. Indeed, the fact that the dance took on a wildness and she could transport herself away from reality increased its import. For this brief evening workshop at Coconino Community College outside Flagstaff, Arizona, the ordinary gymnasium floor would become hallowed ground.

As if it were the natural order of things, the men became the drummers and the women the dancers. The men — dressed in various outfits — stood at the drums; the women stood, spread out at arm's length from each other, waiting for Josuf to instruct them in specific dances and rhythms, the vibrations, the earthiness, the abandonment of inhibition, that might arise from the pounding of feet to the pulsing of hand drums in the night-hushed room.

Josuf, well known in African dance circles, had visited the Southwest several times. Now, he was spending a semester as Visiting Professor of African Dance and Drums at Arizona State University. He and his videos were familiar to Rosie. Tonight, his electrifying presence, combined with a wisdom and even gentleness of presentation, engaged her psyche from the inception. She became enveloped in the living, breathing organism of this evening of dance.

The men nodded to each other, looked at Josuf, and continued on. Josuf occasionally gave them a cue, but one of the men from Africa kept the beat and served as lead drummer. They began at one end, rippling toward the other end of the crescent, until all the drummers were playing.

The drums picked up in speed and sound, resonant and pulsing, with intertwined rhythms. Occasionally there would be a change. A student of both piano and dance in college, Rosie listened for the rhythm and cadence. At first she heard fugal rhythms, with a few drums beating to the "1, 2, 3 and 4 and," then the next group entering on the first group's "3, 4" with a "1, 2." The drummers created a fugue of four parts. Then Rosie could hear competing rhythms, with one group at a 4/4 count, but another group with an indiscernible beat. Rosie felt as well as heard their skill as she absorbed the music's complexity.

Josuf stepped forward and back, gesturing all the dancers to move toward him as he moved one foot behind the other, then for them to retreat as he danced forward into their midst. Rosie looked first only at him, then shifted her gaze to the brown/red/gold/azure skirt of the African-American woman diagonally to her right. Soon, though, as if drawn by an invisible magnet, she found herself looking directly at the floor just in front of her as she began to stomp, slide and pace in rhythm with Josuf, the musicians, and the multicolored chorus of women dancers.

There were a few musical numbers from specific regions, each a few minutes long. Then, after some words from Josuf, the drummers embarked on a series of cadences that waved, pounded, and continued to throb. Rosie no longer needed to look at anyone or anything. She swayed. She stomped. She felt her center, her core, drawing closer to the earth. She felt her hair dampening at the nape of her neck, a few rivulets of perspiration moving down her face and between her breasts. A sense of freedom flowed from her groin down her legs and shimmered out through her arms to her fingertips. When the mood invited her, she shook her shoulders and fanny and raised her face as if to the sun.

Others swayed in sensual synchronization. Rosie glanced across the room to see waves of reds, yellows and blues flowing as one, bodies moving in a chorus. Some women had taken off blouses and let their breasts move freely. Wide white-toothed smiles accompanied the movements, as if mere dance was delivering these women from a place of bondage to a field of freedom.

Rosie smelled the sweat of the many heated bodies swaying and stomping, the scent of dirty feet against the wood-beamed gym floor. Yet the smells mattered little. What mattered at this moment in time was the beat, the swirling colors, the heat, the passion, the harmony in numbers, as drummers and dancers spoke to each other in the language of movement and sound. She had come here to dance in preparation for her recital at the end of the semester. It was early December, cold and dark outside, seemingly unpropitious for anything close to a vibrant African dance dress rehearsal. She had come feeling tight, even apprehensive.

Yet here it was, the full experience; public yet intimate, close yet expanding; hot; gathered yet disseminated. The sounds she had heard dozens of times before combining anew to become a vehicle of transport. Rosie let herself follow the beat, the rhythm, the shushuring of the dancers' feet and skirts. She lost track of time and place. As if in a dream, she saw herself on the earth in a faraway place, maybe at night, maybe in West Africa, maybe not even of this world. Her emotions ruled her moves and she went into a trance, with her conscious mind not awake, but her core remaining in touch with the ground, the beat, those around her, and the parameters of place. She felt pure and impure, dirty and washed, in control of her destiny and unable to change it, step-sliding and hip-swiveling in what seemed an unending frenzy.

The drummers wrapped it up in a slick cadence and a crescendo of all drums in sync. They suddenly stopped. The auditorium burst into applause, every member of the group clapping and laughing. Rosie awoke. She was drenched in sweat. But the gaunt old drummer was there, again appearing to look her way. What was it that lured her, yet so quickly destroyed the freedom she had felt just moment before? A shiver racked her body. An old anxiety returned, cellular memory triggered by the swarthy stranger in the drum circle.

Josuf was saying kind, professorial and complimentary things to the entire class of performers — amateur, student and professional alike. He spoke about some occasions coming together in a special communion. He said he had felt it here tonight, here in this off-the-main-road Coconino County Community College gym. He mentioned a few women in specific outfits (not knowing people by name). Rosie's sienna, teal and ochre skirt was among those praised. She, in fact, did stand out for excellence. She was good at this dance, because she so desperately needed it. She danced, she knew, to escape memories from the past, from the room, from despair. Like a lion in the savannah, the dance promised a momentary freedom from the uncertainty of never knowing when the feelings, the persistent fear, would return and overwhelm her.

None of this internal whirlwind showed to the outside world in the face of the twenty-four-year-old woman with curly mahogany hair, wrapped in a vibrant Nigerian skirt.

At the moment that the applause swelled for Josuf, the drummers and the dancers, she knew she would go to the family farm in the mountains.

Chapter 2

D anny hauled the suction dredge from under the porch and nudged it with a boot. Since he and his sister Rosie were now in charge, he thought he'd take up seeking gold in "that thar crik" as the early miners might say. He studied the dredge in the low angle of December's afternoon light. The equipment consisted of a metal sluice box, about four feet square, four inches deep; a motor; and a series of hoses. The bottom of the sluice box was a heavily laced metal sieve for catching heavy rocks — for catching *gold*.

Tall and softly stocky, with irregular straw-gold hair and a trimmed-up beard, Danny loosened his dark parka. He'd prepared for a stiff wind-chill factor, but the mountains were silent and the slanting afternoon sun warmed everything it touched. His open jacket revealed loose boot-cut jeans with a silver buckle accenting the tooled leather belt.

His fingers gently traveled each piece of equipment. He fondly let drop a forefinger against the ribbed edges of the hoses. He cupped his palm around the smooth corners of the motor. His boot toed the sluice box lying on the ground.

"So," he spoke after some silence, "shall we carry it to the creek, Hotchkiss?" His best friend from Flagstaff had come along, a seasoned lover of the woods, and another slightly serious, slightly self-deprecating would-be prospector.

Hotchkiss was shorter, with a slight build, but clean-shaven, to make up for the slightly crooked teeth that could never have afforded an orthodontist. A scar above his left eye from a fall gave Hotchkiss a slightly sinister appearance, quite a contradiction to his amiable attitude.

"I'd say wait until spring, Danny." Hotchkiss replied, momentarily the more rational of the two. " We don't have much time on this trip. It's pretty cumbersome to set the dredge into the right spot in the creek. Takes a bit of an effort. And we couldn't leave it there. Anyone could come along and use it for their own purposes or steal it right out of the water."

"Makes sense. Let's take a look at the creek, though. Been pretty dry the past few years. I wonder where there will be a good spot to lay her down. See that fallen tree over there?"

Danny knew he was entertaining a fantasy. Even though there was some money from their parents' estate, he couldn't just abandon work in Flagstaff and live out here at the cabin in the Bradshaws for several months. He'd have to schedule some weekends off work to make his mining adventure worthwhile. During the slow months in March and April he could get a few more days off–after the winter skiers in Flagstaff had abandoned the muddy slopes of Mt. Agassiz and disappeared from local coffee shops, and before desert escapees and alpine hikers of summer replaced them. But, for now, just getting the dredge into working order and ready to set in the creek come spring would suffice.

Only a year and a half had passed since Mom and Dad had died suddenly on the Interstate-17 in a six-car pile-up, as they were heading down the "hill," the two and a half hour drive to Scottsdale and a descent from over seven thousand feet altitude among the Ponderosa, to barely fifteen hundred feet and the sweltering floor of the desert. Flagstaff was a bustling tourist town in the summer months. Everyone joked about the "dry heat," but they'd all escape to the mountains when they could.

Danny had just graduated from Northern Arizona University and Rosie had finished her junior year at a small college in

Prescott. They had both already taken a year off in the middle of their college lives to pursue "real-world experience," or a "walkabout," as Rosie had liked to call it. Just some work and travel. But he had returned, finished up at NAU, and had been planning to settle in Flagstaff. Rosie had returned from her "walkabout" at several organic farms in Europe, in time for her junior year. She had come up the hill to Flagstaff as well, visiting for a few days before returning to Prescott.

Then, the summer before her senior year in college, came the crash.

The four of them — Mom, Dad, Rosie and Danny — had all spent the morning together hiking in Buffalo Soldier Park at the foot of the snow-capped San Francisco Peaks. They'd all gone to Danny's restaurant for lunch. Danny took over a short shift as Mom and Dad headed back to Scottsdale, and Rosie had gone to Danny's house to pack up.

Danny had just walked in the door after the late lunch clean-up when the phone rang. Somehow he and Rosie had known, even at the first ring, that something was wrong. Not what was wrong, just that something was.

"Danny?"

His chest tightened. "Yes?"

"It's me, Uncle Phil." A pause. "Danny, there's been an accident. A car crash. A pile-up coming down the Black Canyon Highway from Cordes Junction. A truck's brakes went out and the driver lost control. Your parents... there were six cars..."

"Mom and Dad?" Danny knew the answer.

"They — they were killed instantly. Oh, Danny, I'm so sorry." Uncle Phil started to break down on the phone, then composed himself. "I called you first. Do you want to call Rosie, or should I?"

"Hold on a sec, Uncle Phil." Danny could hardly breathe. He felt suspended in time, the air leaden, the room stifling. He tried taking a gulp of air and letting it out. Tried staving off a wave of tears that would arrive once he was off the phone. Yet somehow the scent of stale coffee grounds in the kitchen hit his nostrils and stuck. Finally he could answer.

"Rosie's here, Uncle Phil."

"Oh, my God. I'll tell her. Put her on."

Danny handed the phone to Rosie. But, like Danny, she too already knew. After listening silently for a few minutes, Rosie murmured something and returned the phone to Danny. His mind hit that autopilot of requirements that must be met when a crisis hits. He started thinking of what must be done, immediately, and then what next and what next.

"Uncle Phil, I need to call my work and square away some time off. I'll need to get several folks to cover shifts. I have to tell my roommates. They'll need to take care of the dogs." He paused, about to choke up and flailing wildly about in his mind for what was being forgotten. He couldn't think of anything else. "Then we'll come straight home. We'll go to our house. We'll be there tonight."

He put the phone back in Rosie's hand, seeking in her eyes if she had anything more to say. Her chin tensed, her eyes steeled. She studied him intensely and then inhaled to the full capacity of her lungs. As if there would be no air left at the end of her next sentence. She placed the phone close to her ear.

"Uncle Phil, this is Rosie again. I'll call my college. I'll come home with Danny. We'll be there tonight. And, Uncle Phil?"

"Yes?"

"Did they suffer?"

"No, Rosie, they didn't suffer. They didn't know what hit them."

Rosie took command after that. She put out suitcases that would hold formal wear and changes of clothes for a week. She scanned Danny's bedroom for pictures or memorabilia he'd want for this stay. She walked briskly to the kitchen, tossed the stale grounds into a lidded bin and brewed green tea for them both for the ride down the mountain. She queried him on whether they'd left anything undone. Her heightened composure stood at odds with the chaos she felt inside.

They arrived at their parent's Scottsdale home by seven

16

in the evening. Uncle Phil and other family folks were there. Many hugs were exchanged, many tears shed and several memories shared with sadness. Someone went out for pizza. Even with trauma, they would need to eat. Finally, Danny and Rosie were left alone, exhausted. They slept in the living room, together, fighting the widening fear of abandonment.

Danny had accompanied Uncle Phil the next day to identify the bodies, and, a few days after that, together with Rosie, they had picked up the cremains. They numbly participated in settling details for the memorial service.

Danny hadn't been able to read Rosie's emotions immediately after their parents died. She had been uncharacteristically calm during all the days immediately following that grim hour when they both got the news — that both their parents were dead.

At the memorial service, Rosie had spoken just a few well-measured phrases, calm but equivocal, disconnected. When it was Danny's turn, he tried to muster carefully chosen words to say that wouldn't bring on a cascade of emotions and embarrass everyone there.

Then there were the sympathetic but practical meetings with Mr. Sawyer, the trustee of the estate, and the details of how to handle income that was not a huge amount but, nonetheless, had to be "managed." Danny and Rosie could have a modest monthly cash flow, but the properties were to remain in the trust for the time being.

Danny had hardly heard anything that Mr. Sawyer said. His head had felt full of clanging cathedral bells, silent but filling every available space that the sound of a human voice might reach. Rosie appeared to pay far more attention than he when they went over the details of the trust. It was she who asked if the house in Scottsdale was still available to live in, what was happening to the farm in the Bradshaws, whether any money would flow on a regular basis. Who was in charge of the family trust? What were she and Daniel supposed to do? Were they in charge of anything at all? How did it fit together? Did anything go to *him*? Would *he* have any part of the estate, would *he* have any right to go to the Scottsdale house or the farm? Any right to contact them?

Mr. Sawyer took in Rosie's avalance of questions and responded slowly but with abundant clarity and compassion.

"No, Rosie, he will get nothing. Your parents specifically excluded him — your adopted brother — from the will. They obtained a Court Injunction against him to prevent any further contact with either one of you. I don't think they had time — and maybe not the courage — to tell you, but they did tell me when they were making revisions to the trust how profound was their regret at how things had turned out. How they had meant to adopt an older brother who would be an integral part of the family. How they thought that 'physically healthy' meant no emotional baggage. How from the outset he caused problems. How ashamed they were to learn they had not protected you, Rosie, from sexual abuse. And you, Danny, too. You had been a real happy kid before he dominated the family dynamics."

After a pause. Mr. Sawyer concluded.

"This was a secret they were too ashamed to share. But they told me as they revised everything to exclude him. I believe you should know. He gets nothing. He can't come near you."

By then Daniel knew that *his* name would probably not cross her lips aloud ever again. But the elephant of *his* absence in the discussions contrasted eerily with Rosie's superficially calm elucidation of issues that required clarity and resolution. He'd come by this heightened awareness when he and Rosie were just kids, when Dad was at work and Mom might go out to the store, just for a few minutes. When the abuse began. Sometimes his older brother would pick on him. That hurt. But it wasn't just the bullying, the belittling. It wasn't even the fear of getting beat up, his brother's idea of fun.

No, it was the fear that something was happening to Rosie, something he didn't quite understand and couldn't stop, when the door slammed in his face and he was told they'd both get killed if he told his parents.

And Rosie had come by it too, at the same time, when she

listened in fear that *he'd* get her into her room, and he'd pin her down, cover her mouth, and touch her privates. When she prayed that Mom or Dad could hear something, come save her, fearing after his threats that he really would kill her, or Danny, or Mom and Dad. That heightened cellular apprehension when something devastating has begun and she couldn't control any of what happened to her.

For Danny, it was also the sense of betrayal that he couldn't escape, even here, now, almost twenty years later, over a hundred miles away. That time long ago when he'd happily welcomed his new, adopted brother with innocent enthusiasm, only to have this powerful kid turn on him. It was the ongoing sense that he could never measure up, never be as good an athlete, never be as strong, no matter how hard he had tried.

And finally, he felt an ongoing shame that he could not protect his little sister, that he couldn't save her from the one who never acted like a real brother anyway.

In the end, the steps were simplified to an immediate transfer into Danny's and Rosie's separate trust accounts and quarterly conference calls to keep things on track.

They took the next semester to live together in the Scottsdale home that held so many memories, to get jobs and sell the house, and become used to being orphans. Adults, yes, but orphans nonetheless. Yes, there were uncles and aunts, but despite all their emotions about a rocky childhood, Danny and Rosie both felt completely bereft. Staying in the house, staring at old family photos, paintings, Navajo rugs from Mom and Dad's collection, sitting in Dad's armchair, using Mom's inherited silverware for every meal, seemed to postpone the inevitable admission they both had to accept. Their parents were dead. It was now just them.

After Christmas in Scottsdale with aunts and uncles and the sale of the house at the end of the year, Danny took some of his favorite furniture and moved to Flagstaff, rented a house, and took in some roommates to share costs. He'd been able to maintain friendly contact with his old boss and went back to work at the restaurant. After a few months he became manager. He and the owner were looking to expand the operation and become business partners.

Rosie had returned to college for her senior year in January. Danny had fallen into a pattern of calling her weekly to check up, listen, and be the older brother he felt he hadn't been very good at before. That past autumn in Scottsdale, he had learned the specific ugly secrets that haunted her. The repeated molestations. The secrecy. The threats. Danny became aware of how the abuse affected him too. They had never talked about it until after the crash, until they lived alone together in the house. After a few months they called it, between themselves, "the haunted house" and were glad to move out and leave its childhood pain behind. At least they thought they left it behind.

The past year and a half back in Flagstaff had been pretty much on emotional hold–up each morning before dawn for the early shift, biking to work, watching golf tournaments on TV with the roommates (a sport he didn't even play), cooking dinner for the house most nights, doing dishes, watching more TV, sleep and up the next day. No girlfriends, no adventures, no thoughts, just a bleak repetitiveness over the months. Until he and Hotchkiss came up with the idea of dredging for gold. The family had a dredge, but it hadn't been used for years. Reviving a hobby that Dad loved struck a resonant chord, gave a sense of purpose that had been missing since his parents' death.

Danny and Hotchkiss walked over to the creek, ambled up- and downstream for about an hour surveying prospecting possibilities. They were seeking a solid "elbow" in the creek, maybe carved out by previous storms, where heavy metals would tend to settle near the bend, caught in an eddy and dropped to the bottom of the pool. That was the most likely place to find bits of gold that had been water-carved out of a vein in the mountainside and that had traveled in a fast-flowing stream to settle, maybe to be found by the sidekick miners. They found two likely spots, and then returned to the house.

"Want to stay the night?" Hotchkiss leaned over to haul in some cut walnut and pine for the indoor fireplace.

"Sure, we've got the food."

Danny pitched in on the firewood. Soon they had a fire roaring and the living room warmed up from forty-five to about sixty degrees. They chugged a few beers and let the coals settle, then threw steaks on the grill and opened a bag of chips.

"Hotchkiss," Danny started, watching the embers char the fatty edges of the sirloin, "you've known me and Rosie for a couple of years now. I don't know what she has in mind, but I'm suspecting that she's going to want to come up here. I don't know. She hasn't said anything. She's avoided stating any plans. She's come out here with friends from Prescott several times. They're a lot of organic types. Her graduation is in less than two weeks. I wouldn't be surprised if she wanted to do some farming here."

Hotchkiss nursed a second beer. They had brought Bud because aluminum cans were lighter and safer than glass, bumping along a rocky Forest Service road. But Bud didn't entice you to drink too much. Just not in the same class as a good bottled micro-brew.

"You know I lived on a farm in Chino Valley when I was a kid, right, Dan?"

"Yeah, I seem to remember ..."

"Well, it was hard but I liked it. I liked the cattle, the chickens, the crops, the harvesting. If it wasn't so hard to break even, I'd have tried to figure out a way to stay there."

Danny forked the meat and flipped both pieces. A burst of flame licked the sides. He inhaled a whiff of the medium-rare beef on the grill.

"She's a tough cookie, Danny, she's at this college where they study the environment. I'd say if there's anyone who could pull it off here, she could. She'd need some help, but it could work."

"But I'm supposed to look after my little sister," Danny said, knowing his objection was halfhearted.

"You know she's more likely to make it here than you are. You really didn't go for the outdoors the same way. No hunting, no farm experience. You've always been more into business. Didn't she work on a farm somewhere along the line?"

"A year on farms in Europe, yeah, you're right."

"And you're not so far away that you can't check in on her?"

"Right."

"So what's the harm in trying?"

"Steaks are done, Hotchkiss. Let's get 'em off the grill before they become charcoal." Danny put the discussion to bed and forked the slabs onto separate plates.

The farmhouse hosted a small collection of guitars, a banjo and hand drums. After dinner Danny strummed while Hotchkiss tapped out a few Country Western 'done her wrong' songs. They laughed at their fake twangs and hit the sack.

In the morning, over eggs and bacon, Danny asked, "Any last thoughts?"

"What?" Hotchkiss laughed. "On Rosie? The creek? Gold? Christmas?"

Danny relaxed. *I can't run the whole show, can I?* he thought to himself.

"Okay, I get it. Maybe I don't have to work so hard at being a big brother. Let's pack up and go."

He clapped Hotchkiss on the shoulder. They doused the fire, locked up, drove out of the Bradshaws on the rutted forest road and arrived back in Flagstaff in two hours.

Rosie spent the night at Danny's after the African dance, grateful for his brotherly warmth, for his quiet way of not asking a lot of questions. She was deeply startled by both the sensual passion that arose within her, moving with the other women to the throbbing of the drums, and the undefined fright triggered by the old drummer. It threatened to shake her foundations. Though she couldn't figure out why. She pushed the feeling below the surface and focused on the Lab, the Pitt Bull, and the German shepherd puppy that greeted her as she let herself in.

"Hey, dogs." She patted each one vigorously, familiar with them from her many surfings on the household couch. "Hey, Danny." She gave her brother a grateful hug. He was big and burly and, honestly, the only masculine comfort she trusted just now. And missing Dad was huge. They held each other a bit longer than usual.

"Beer?"

"Actually, a big glass of water would fit the bill right now. That class was a serious workout." She shivered again, involuntarily.

Danny noticed the quivering.

"Catching a cold? Something happen at the class? You seem a bit off, Sis. What's up?"

"Nothing, nothing. Just tired, that's all. Josuf Mbwana is a fabulous teacher. He really gets folks going. I love how he draws not only us college- types, but the older black women in the community. And his lead drummer must have a special magic. There was a point, Dan, when several of the women just took off their tops and really let it shake. With snow outside! You would have had quite an eye-fest."

She was glad to have a point of reference to divert him from probing questions.

"How about you, Rosie? If I'd been there, would I have been embarrassed? Would I have had to protect you from the drummers?"

In a flash, the darkness returned. Rosie fended it off.

"No, Dan, I was wearing a leotard bodysuit. Couldn't possibly have stripped the top off without removing everything. That would been a show-stopper. I behaved."

Although Rosie thought of how it might be, to be in a safe place, in a field perhaps, with a hundred African women and all the drummers Senegalese, just the pulsing of the beat and the quickening of her libido. It seemed like such a delicious luxury, one that lured and terrified her at the same time. It was as if African dance was the only means to express herself, to tap into her inner sensuality that was safe. A place where she couldn't be hurt.

After a quick shower, Rosie returned to the living room wrapped in a quilt, smelling lightly of lavender, and sat on the aging leather couch, paws on her thighs, as Danny handed her another glass. The spell, while clear in memory, was over. Danny matched her water with mint tea, stuff they had harvested from the creek last summer. "Off the hard stuff until Christmas," he commented as he, too, gave the dogs attention.

They were actually the roommates' dogs, but Danny and Rosie were like family, so to speak, to the affectionate canines.

"So, Rosie, you're about to wrap it up with college. Congrats. What's the date of graduation? December sixteenth? It'll be strange not having a little sister in college anymore. Then you'll officially be 'grown up'. I won't be able to boss you around like when we were kids. He flashed inwardly on last weekend's conversation with Hotchkiss at the farm. "Got any ideas of what next?"

"Hey, Danny, let's take it one step at a time," Rosie parried, staving off a serious conversation about her "future." Danny sometimes just acted a bit too much like a parent. Something she wasn't sure she could handle right now. She did not want to talk about her idea, not until she was sure she had more pieces in place.

"Sooo, graduation is December sixteenth, Saturday, at the Yavapai College auditorium. Please come. I have room for you to stay overnight at my place. There'll be a party afterward. Then it'll take me a few days to wrap it up, pack stuff, and then, is it okay if I come back to Flag for Christmas? I really don't have plans yet, and last Christmas with the relatives in Phoenix was sort of a downer. I'd really rather stay here with you and your friends."

"I hoped you'd like that idea. I feel the same way. Wish Mom and Dad were here. But they're not. And the relatives just sort of remind me ..." Danny drifted in thought for a moment. "Some of the roommates are leaving for Christmas break, so the house won't be as busy, but I'm dog sitting. And several folks in town are looking to have a barbecue. It'll be good."

They turned in early, he on the futon in his bedroom with the puppy at his feet. Rosie took the living room couch, and the other two canines kept guard. Danny was up and out by 5:45 in the morning for work, so she didn't have to say much. She stopped by his restaurant for pancakes and coffee and was soon on the road back to Prescott.

Chapter 3

D amn. The December cold bit into him like shrapnel. An early but old snow lay on the ground, mainly dirt-shoveled heaps against the sides of streets and icy lumps under the bushes below the building's fascia. But at least he was warm. Wainwright's current apartment complex, sandwiched between Route 66 and the railroad tracks in Flagstaff, had central heating. It was all efficiencies and one bedrooms, harboring a motley collection of men who had all seen better days and many years. Wainwright looked out his dingy front window, through crooked bare oak branches, assessing the wind chill factor and the availability of pale sunlight. He pulled up his old fatigues over worn longjohns and added a flannel jacket over the grungy T-shirt that had served as pajamas. He ground out the cigarette he had started while still in bed, piled it on top of a full ashtray, nostrils dulled to the smell of stale smoke settling in the room, and lit up another.

He'd worked on his ammunition all morning. One of the things that could keep him sane was making bullets– mainly .45s and .38s. His favorite was the .45s for the sidearm he had been issued in Vietnam in the '60s. All the supplies were arranged precisely on the shelves near the workbench: the casings, the heads, and the powder. On the workbench was clamped the machine that would alternately hold the scale for measuring powder and the rotating turrets for each caliber-size of rounds. In fact, he had turned the bedroom into an arsenal factory and slept on a secondhand futon in the living room in front of the TV. If he kept it on all night, his mushy brain might not have room for the nightmares. He just absorbed the late-night talk shows and watched the 24-hour movie channel. Kept his mind off of it.

Captain Alden Thoreau Wainwright, Marine Air. Vietnam vet. A Bronze Star, a Purple Heart, the Distinguished Service Medal, and an honorable discharge over thirty years ago. And PTSD. The constant rain of antiaircraft chatter, then the 'copter crash, and later, the human cinders, took their toll. But the worst, actually, were the nightmares. The main one was the crash when his best friend Tom went down. First, the explosion, then the fire, the searing, acrid smell of explosives and blood, then having to do "search and rescue," a euphemism for collecting the remains of the corpses inside. Then having to help put the pieces of bodies burned to a crisp into body bags, and label them so everyone got a bag. So every family had someone to mourn. Tom's tags had been discovered, but the rest was unrecognizable. Then they had to zip them up and send them back stateside for interment. Sometimes the dream was just an explosion. Other times, Wainwright became the body pieces and would wake in a sweat as the body bag was being zipped over his face. Night after F-ing night. That's how come there was the TV and the late-night movies.

And music by day. What had started as an obsession with acid rock had morphed into more eclectic tastes. You could go to Macy's café and hear some self-styled country-western balladeers strumming with an amp, or you could hit the Weatherford Hotel and listen to anything from Celtic to rock-'n'-roll. Summers, he'd found the street players revisiting classic folk protest stuff.

Then, one afternoon last July, he'd encountered the drum

circle on the plaza on the weekends. For some reason, it grabbed him. Maybe the simplicity of hand drums. Maybe the testosterone of the guys in the circle. Maybe the vibes, the steady rhythm, sometimes varying, but consistently filling the void, and in the end coming back home together.

So Wainwright had wandered down to Route 66 and east of Butler to one of the pawnshops downtown. The owner thought there might be an African drum.

"Go look over there in the musical instruments section. Or in the folk imports corner with the baskets and weavings and fertility statues."

The drum lay nestled among other drums and guitar cases, kind of a primitive standout among the technologically tweaked options of the U.S. music industry. Wainwright picked it up, tapped the skin, approached the owner. Pulled a pistol out from under his heavy olive jacket.

"Got a pistol from 'Nam, a Chi Com 7.62 x 25 mm automatic you might want. Chinese took over production after the Soviets quit producing their T-33 around 1954. You can tell it's Chinese by the serrations and Chinese ideograms on the grip. Used a lot by VC and NVA officers. Got it in a market. Kept it in perfect working order."

"Could use one of those. Collectors around here want one of everything." The fellow behind the counter fingered the metal, put both hands on the grip, pointing down and away, toward a pile of Navajo blankets, a finely woven black, red, gray and white Storm Pattern rug on the top. "Lock's in place. Loaded?"

"Course not." Wainwright retook possession to show it was empty. "Mostly for show. But load it up and it could be used to kill someone, easy."

They made the swap; the owner getting what he thought was by far the better deal. But Wainwright had a dozen more where the pistol came from–and now, one hand drum. Something began to feel hopeful in his chest. For the first time in a long time, his footsteps didn't scuff.

He held the drum by a leather thong and walked around town. He stayed on the north side of the railroad tracks and

Route 66, avoiding the Northern Arizona University campus that had been his means to fend off the draft for four years. It was at NAU, in his senior year, that he had met Jean, compact and self-reliant, with a long dark braid that stuck out from under her winter wool hat or pushed through her Route 66 ball cap in the spring.

He'd fallen in love with Jean almost instantly during the fall of 1961. She seemed so clear, so caring, so determined. She was a double major in English and Spanish, planning to become an ESL or Bilingual Ed teacher in an inner city school in Phoenix. Wainwright walked past the crystal store. The scent of jasmine incense wafted out the front door. The same incense Jean would light when they stayed at her place sharing glasses of wine and hopes for the future.

He recalled now how the flower's redolence attached itself to her hair and clothes. He had lost himself in Jean's exotic aroma almost the entire year.

The spring of 1962 had resounded with joy and dread. Joy at losing himself in her loving embrace. Dread that the draft loomed in June. The Vietnam War was heating up. President Kennedy seemed convinced that, with the vacuum created by the French departure and aggression of the Chinese in the north, the Communists would take over all of Southeast Asia. If drafted, Wainwright would wind up in the infantry in Vietnam. The Army route almost guaranteed you'd become cannon fodder.

Instead, upon graduating in May, he took the leap and joined the Marines to avoid the Army. In the USMC, he could, as a college graduate, enter officer candidate school. He aimed for Marine Air, completed OCS as a Second Lieutenant, and went to 'Nam as a helicopter pilot.

It was also the toughest branch of the service. He would prove himself as tough and brave as his father had been, a pilot in the Pacific during World War II. He'd be one of them: "The few. The proud. The Marines."

Until the whiff of jasmine, Wainwright had completely forgotten the ambrosial air of Jean's body. He still struggled, after so many years, to remember her face. At least he could recall the perfume and hold on to one good memory.

When he'd returned from his 13-month year in Viet Cong territory and the full three years of active duty, Jean had become a teacher in a South Phoenix elementary school, teaching English as a Second Language to the predominantly Mexican and Central American immigrants. She had waited for him. They married quickly and thought they could make it. He never talked about what he'd seen, what had hit him, what war really was.

Wainwright stuffed it. He tried to suppress all his memories, anxiety and flashbacks. He got a job teaching aviation at a community college. The shrapnel still in his leg eliminated actual flying from the opportunities normally available to a vet with his training and experience.

He thought he would like teaching. Serving as a pilot had become imbedded in his sense of self. But there would be days when he just couldn't focus. The littlest thing – a falling pencil, a shuffling foot – would distract him. The nightmares and flashbacks persisted. Jean couldn't help but notice when he'd sit bolt upright in the middle of the night drenched in sweat. She urged him to go to the VA.

So he went. You'd think that in the monolithic complex at 7th Street and Indian School in Phoenix there'd be good counseling for vets. But it was spotty. They treated him as a failure, not a Marine who'd served with distinction in a war. He would drop out of the group, return, and after two or three tries, he gave up altogether. "Fuck the VA."

It took a few years, but eventually too many people noticed that he missed days of work. Faculty had to cover. Students complained. He couldn't pull together assignments or grade tests. Finally someone more reliable replaced him.

He buried his pain in alcohol. At first he pretended a glass of wine was enough. That's what Jean would drink, mainly on weekends. But quickly he had resorted to scotch, bourbon or gin to kill the pain, the memories. But all of them brought with them the side effects of horrendous hangovers. Finally he resorted mostly to vodka and beer, with the fewest morning effects. Got so every night he'd down almost a fifth.

Jean had tried to get him to stop, to go to AA. She simply hadn't a clue about the torment stored in every cell of his body, torment that begged for release, for forgetfulness, for peace. One night, in a drunken rage, he shoved her against the couch and threw the Smirnoff against the wall, spattering vodka and shards of glass across the room.

The next day Jean was gone. Left a note: "I can't take it any more." A few days later, a knock on the door and divorce papers were served.

It was a blessing that Arizona was a no-fault state. No matter what anyone said, it was easier to bear knowing that all she said was that there were "irreconcilable differences and no likelihood of repairing the marriage." When she could have said so much more. He accepted the papers, cried them into a soggy pulp, failed to file a Response, and the marriage was dissolved by default.

Jean had taken all her things, even their wedding photo, so he had no tangible memorabilia, no way to recall her face. Still, her all too brief presence in his life haunted him. Their desperate inability to overcome the war settled, ironically, as one of the happier times he could recall. He'd had Jean in his life. Now life was barren, like the oak branches outside his dirty window.

His coat pulled tight against the December weather, Wainwright walked back west on Route 66 — Main Street — and over toward the Lowell Observatory. Suddenly, he realized he was dog-tired. He scuffed back to his apartment. He microwaved a pot pie for dinner and sat on the futon with his cigs and a six-pack, TV on mute, until he faded out.

The next day, waking stiffly, Wainwright realized it was the day of the African dance thing. Hotchkiss would pick him up in the afternoon and they'd drive out to Coconino Community College. They'd get together with a lot of the guys and this man, Josuf Mbwana, and a room full of women doing African gyrations. Suddenly, he felt hopeful.

He decided to get out.

First, he dipped south of the tracks and picked up a poppy seed bagel at Biff's. Behind the counter, an older fellow with a receding gray hairline above a wrinkled forehead and black eyebrows understood his financial needs. "If we can feed the cops, we can help the vets." No charge. Coffee included.

He continued north on Beaver Street, crossed the tracks and Route 66 and went over to the Plaza on Aspen. It was cold and empty, with dirty snow by the curb and some melted remains on the wooden benches. There was no one there this morning, but he recalled the beginning, last summer, when an informal circle of guys sat on benches or stood with shoulder straps, thub-thubbing their drums. He had found a spot on a concrete bench and started playing with them. Tentative, awkward at first. Most of them were younger. Most of them knew drums. Not all. Some just thought they knew more. Guys. But then some leftover hippy guys materialized, gray ponytails and flip-flops, everyone with a sixties T-shirt and a drum.

Wainwright felt like part of the gang, though he suspected he was the only one who'd seen active duty. The drum circle grew to about twenty guys. Girls would come by, mostly young and lithe, sometimes dance within the circle. Some of the younger guys seemed to be paired up with the girls. Didn't bother him. He was no good for a woman anymore, and besides, they were young enough to be his children, if he'd had any.

At one of their improvisational gigs, one of the younger guys approached him. The kid with the scar, wearing a lumber jacket. "We're gonna be moving out onto a field off of Lake Mary Road next week. You have a ride?"

Guess it was obvious. "No, how come you're moving?" It seemed so convenient in town.

"Some of the guys like to toke up when they play," the guy said, as if Wainwright knew. "Don't want cops looking over our shoulder. I'm Hotchkiss. So, want a ride? I have a truck. I could pick you up here or at your place if it's nearby."

Wainwright was surprised. Mostly folks didn't talk to him. Left him to himself. But he'd played next to this Hotchkiss guy more than once. Seemed sort of low-key, not too pretentious. Okay, he guessed.

"Sure, I could use a ride. My place is on West Corral, between Route 66 and the railroad tracks, west of Milton. I can wait outside. I'll see you coming."

"I'll pick you up. Bring a jacket, it gets cold out there." Hotchkiss tapped a bit on Wainwright's drum "Nice resonance. Good skin, good wood. Well, see you next Thursday at three then, okay?"

Soon they were truck pals, heading out and back to the circle in the meadow south of the Lake Mary Road. Jam sessions lengthened as several folks passed joints, a few favored wineskins, and generally the music loosened up.

Wainwright had never tried pot. In 'Nam, in the Marines, there was an unspoken code. No drugs. The movies about the war made it seem like everyone did it. Some, mainly Army, found stuff. But in the USMC alcohol was served almost free to the men. Even now, drugs just didn't feel comfortable. But he felt ok taking a squirt from the leather skin filled with Chianti.

At one of the sessions in October someone circulated a poster about an African dance workshop, asking for volunteers to be drummers to support the dancers. Well, yeah, he was interested. Beat sitting in his smoke-filled one-bedroom place with nothing but the TV, some CDs and a home-fashioned munitions factory to keep him from the thoughts that crept into the edges of his mind. Sometimes he couldn't tell if he had just hallucinated, sometimes not sure whether what he saw was a mirage or real. The fallen trees on the hill–were they bodies? The dirt in the streets after a snow–cinders after the crash?

Hotchkiss leaned toward him.

"I can pick you up, Dubya."

Wainwright started. How'd this guy know his nickname from the local bar? He used to be proud to have that other

President's nickname. Not any longer. Not when he realized what a waste all these wars had been and the VA didn't believe he had a service-related injury.

"Hey, my name'..." Wainwright started.

"Yeah, I know. But I think Dubya is kind of friendly. Didn't think you'd mind." Hotchkiss blew it off. "So, Dubya, I sometimes jam with some friends–mix of guitars and drums, sometimes a bass. We might hang out a coupla times. This workshop they're advertising is in December. There's a month beforehand. Got a phone number?"

"Nah, damn cell phones." Had one. They cut it off. "But just knock on Number 5. I'll be waiting."

During the next month Hotchkiss stopped by a few times and took him over to a friend's house–Danny, who played guitar. Another guy came by and played bass. Sometimes they'd all do some hand drums and get a little high. Felt good to be with people. To get high, drag on his Camels while they toked, have a few beers; get a buzz on, with others to distract him. Maybe the bodies, maybe the cinders, maybe the wreckage wouldn't drive him nuts.

So he had looked forward to the thing in December. Now, tonight, Hotchkiss would pick him up for the drum/dance event outside of town. Even though it was bitingly cold outside, he felt warm with anticipation. Good to see the guys again. Good to play together. Good to get out.

Hotchkiss picked him up after sundown, and they drove south a bit and out to the community college. Not far from the Lake Mary Road outings. He brought his drum–the resonant companion from the pawnshop. It fit right in with the others. This African teacher guy, Josuf Mbwana, was lanky, with graying hair and a soft rasping voice. Kindly, as if the man had seen beyond hardships. More like a man who knew the seasons would offer new crops, new beneficence. Good feeling about this guy, Josuf. He joined the circle, near Hotchkiss, and began tapping with the others. Josuf tried them out on a few slow rhythms, then faster ones, and then beats with

34

intricacy and counterpoint. Damn, this was cool. He began playing and looked up for Josuf's lead.

But, way in the back, what was that movement of color? There was this little brown-haired girl, blue eyes, crazy African skirt — like everyone else — but somehow she stood out. What, who did she remind him of? There, she looked back at him! Wainwright tried to look away, looked back at her, then shook his mind back to Josuf. The first number began, and then, for the next hour, he was with the beat. He felt it inside of him, the smell of the leather skins and wood, the sweat of the men, all around the semicircle, with the American guys, the African guys — old and young. They were in sync, offering a pulsing drumbeat to the women dancing back and forth, on the wooden gymnasium floor.

At the end he looked again. There she was! Why did she look at him? She seemed to know him. And he felt like maybe he knew her. But he didn't get why. Something uncomfortably familiar. When Hotchkiss dropped him off a little later, the memory of the circle was pushed aside by the discomfort of the colorful skirt, the dark-brown hair and the piercing blue eyes. Downing some Smirnoff, he endured another night of fitful sleep.

Chapter 4

As Rosie drove down the mountain, bypassing Sedona, and across the Cherry Road turnoff toward Prescott on a flat mesa of high chaparral, she put her mind into high gear. Over the past few years, she had taken a number of friends out to the farm in the Bradshaw Mountains. Over numerous beers and tokes a lot of ideas had surfaced, from panning for gold, to raising cattle (as had been done long ago by previous owners), to running a yoga retreat, to growing vegetables, to raising heirloom hens and selling organic eggs at the Farmers Market. Her best friend Arielle was also finishing up in December, and several guys in their group were graduates, dropouts or friends of someone she knew. There seemed to be a lot of genuine interest in making a go of a sustainable farm. And she had the farm. No rent, no landlord (except herself, and Danny, sort of). It seemed pretty workable.

It would be best for about four or five of them to live there, given all the work they envisioned. Rosie saw Tony and Arielle as a likely duo, and she sort of hoped Chris would be interested. Sort of, because part of her found him outright sexy. But only sort of, because she suspected he had at least one girlfriend at any one time and she didn't want to be hurt.

Another guy, Sam, had finished up last May and stuck around, doing odd jobs for a local farm. There were some others she felt less enthusiastic about, namely a guy called Jack. There were also some she didn't know very well, including a med-tech student named Benny who appeared to be Navajo, and Chloe, a Yavapai County Extension Service field representative who seemed glued to Professor Pete from the college. She could be useful but hers was a real day job, so she wasn't a likely full-time candidate.

Rosie pulled into the gravel drive of her rental house a few blocks off the town square. She put her stuff away in the overcrowded closet, started a load of laundry, checked her e-mails, and flipped open her calendar. The next five days would be a snowstorm of handing in papers and making the final presentation in her African dance program. Then she'd have to go through the drill of graduation. She made a list on a legal pad and then called Arielle.

"Whatcha doing tonight, girlfriend?" she asked after the preliminaries.

"We're going to the Kokopelli Pub for pizza and beers. Want to join us? Tony will be off work in a bit. Meet you there at eight?"

Rosie lay down but couldn't sleep. The idea of going to the mountains seeped into her full consciousness, taking on more and more shape. A blizzard of ideas assailed her, gently but forcefully, like the first wet, cold snow. It could be a farm. It could have chickens. They could grow specialty veggies. Maybe even mushrooms in the fallen oak logs. It could be a remote forest study-station for some of the college students looking for a work-study experience. If they built a platform in the clearing at the top of the hill, she could use her experience and certification in yoga instruction to host meditation retreats.

Finally, she decided another hot shower was in order. She let the hot water run against her back for several minutes, then her front, savoring the massage of every drop from the pulsating showerhead. The lingering anxiety from the *purpose* of the dance, and the uncertainty over how Danny would receive her new plan, seemed to vanish down the drain. She grabbed a large, luxuriously soft towel — something of comfort from the family inheritance — and took her time drying off in front of the misty mirror.

Pulling on a parka, boots, scarf and hat, she headed over toward Kokopelli's. Arielle, Tony and Sam were already in a six-person booth. Arielle and Rosie had been friends since the beginning of college. Fair-skinned with weather-pink cheeks accenting her delicate round face, with a frizzy mass of hair poking out from underneath her wool cap, Arielle was even more petite than Rosie. She exuded an aura of gentleness and the need to be cared for by someone, a man, stronger and protective. Arielle did not like making decisions. It worked better for her to let someone else call the shots.

Tony was currently the one. Tony seemed to love having someone to protect, and someone to be in charge of. He was pretty handsome, Rosie guessed, but you could have missed it with the uneven color of his face: white forehead that had been forever protected by a ball cap, a dark nose and cheeks from plenty of sun, white around the eyes from perpetual shades when outside, and a dark, scruffy five-day shadow of a beard. With the hat off inside Kokopelli's, Tony's hair stuck, uncombed around his ears and forehead. Ah, well, he worked hard and seemed to love Arielle. That's what mattered to Rosie.

With them sat Professor Pete, who seemed to live for the company of students. Tanned from years in the outdoors, on the Colorado River and hiking its plateaus, with a gray pony-tail running well-groomed down the outside of his jacket, he looked like he would soon become an aging hippy. He preferred being called Pete — less distant than "Professor" or "Mr."

Pete taught forest ecology and sustainability. He spent a lot of time teamed up with Chloe taking students on field trips and camping out overnight. The fact that he also had a lady friend more or less his own age cut short any doubt about his sexual orientation or predatory interests. He seemed genuinely to have student concerns at heart.

Chloe was pressed beside him. She had angular features, maybe excessively Anglo-Saxon, but with a luxuriously thick blond braid running down the back of her down vest. Despite the winter chill outside, she wore a snug teaberry spagetti-strap top that revealed her cleavage. Even to Rosie, Chloe appeared sensuous in a slim but muscular way. Her green eyes concentrated, for the moment, on the professor. She kept one hand on his thigh. Romantic interest clearly did not slow down at forty.

Arielle slid gracefully around the beveled edge of the heavy-beamed table and gave Rosie a hug. Through her flannel shirt Rosie could feel Ari's small breasts and the slender curve of her backbone. There was no extra padding at all. "How was Josuf?" Arielle asked. "I wish I could have gone."

They sat next to each other like sisters, with Tony on the other side. They had been through three solid years in school together, surrounding the year of the crash and her parents' death, the semester she took off from school to sell the house, and now the wrap-up of a college career. Despite Arielle's ever-present boyfriend, the girls had managed to have a lot of jam-time on their guitars, making up songs, harmonizing and finding others to join them. Rosie would miss her if they had to part ways.

They ordered beers, pizza and salads. Other folks from the college or town came by and pulled up chairs. A healthy mix of twenty-somethings, with a sprinkling of slightly old-ers, would coalesce at familiar spots and generate their own sense of community. Rosie liked it.

After the group buzz about the past few days, news about whether everyone who aimed to graduate in December was passing all courses, any romances or break-ups, and another round or two of drinks, the conversation eventually turned to "What next?"

Pete directed the question around the table. Arielle was targeted as first quizzee. "Well, Pete, I honestly don't know.

My mom wants me to move back to Ohio, but I don't really want to go."

"And I won't let her," Tony interjected, putting a protective (Rosie wondered, possessive?) arm around her. Arielle laughed a little, as if it were settled without more thought.

"Great, Arielle," said Rosie. "Maybe we can hang out more. What will you be doing, Tony?"

"This part-time construction work is getting old. It slows down in the winter. I'm thinking of finding a place where I can work on a farm, raise some goats and chickens."

"And he can start with the ones in our chicken coop," added Arielle. She and Tony had been raising pet laying hens in their back yard for an independent study, documenting feed, warmth and number of eggs per type of hen. "We could order more and make a real profit at Farmers Market."

"That sounds great," Pete added, routinely supportive of student ideas. It was pretty easy to get good grades and comments in his courses. "So, Rosie, do you have any idea what you'll be doing next? You were pretty sharp in those botanical reports you gave. I'd love to see you do graduate work here."

"Actually, I do have an idea," Rosie said, knowing full well that graduate school was always an option. But she also knew the family inheritance was limited and she didn't plan to spend it all before getting out in the world to earn her own keep. "You know our place in the woods? I've been thinking about starting it up this spring as an organic, sustainable farm. "But," she hesitated, "I need some business partners to make it a go. You've all been there. What do you think of investing some time and sweat in a start-up sustainable farm? We could get out there as early as February or March and be planting by April in the greenhouse, or May in the field, have lettuce and radishes and stuff by June, and a run of various crops all summer long. What do y'all think?"

Pete spoke up first. "You sound like you've really give this some serious thought. But the road is kind of rough. Are you sure you can regularly make the drive to Market?"

"Mom and Dad left me a 4X4. It can haul stuff and it

handles the road well. We've moved a lot of stuff to and from without a problem. At least, I've never had a problem," she added.

Truth was, she *had* had problems. Flat tires, dead battery, rain-soaked mudslides. But a few isolated facts should not cloud the promise of a great idea. Rosie was sure this could work. She had the strength, she knew it. She had the knowledge from working in a couple of organic gardens and her field biology major. With a few friends from Prescott — their farm skills and their construction skills — plus a little investment, she could do it. She was sure. And she could get away from the city, her fears, her past — from her fear of *him*.

Sam jumped in first. "I've always wanted to do a start-up, Rosie. That sounds great!"

Tony looked at Arielle. "Whaddya think, Ari? It would make a great opportunity. Virgin soil, heirloom hens, a place to really show what we know?"

Arielle beamed. Tony and Rosie, two of her favorite people. It looked like they had already decided and would take charge. She just had to join in. "When do we get started?"

Rosie was suddenly the one who had to rein everyone in. "It really can't begin until about February or March," she began. "First is graduation, then Christmas and New Year's, and if it snows in January or February the roads can be difficult. But you guys have a place to stay until then, right? And I can surf with either you or Danny." She paused, and then continued a bit dramatically. "I'll have to tell my big brother what the deal is. He's sooo protective."

"Oh, he'll go along with it," Tony answered. "It's a great idea, and basically he knows you can pull it off. Besides, isn't he sort of interested in dredging for gold? I bet we see more of him once we start living on the farm."

Pete wrapped it up. "I think, with the right introductions, we may be able to find some support from the college. Rosie, good idea you have going there. We'll all be glad to help, won't we, Chloe?"

Chloe nodded. Pete liked the idea. And she had a lot of professional expertise to offer on soils, crops, and water.

"Sounds like we have a month or two to put all the plans together, list what's needed, and get supplies. Rosie, if you can stay in town a fair amount of the time," she looked at Tony and Arielle, "you can pull everything together. Give me a call if you need help." She placed her Extension Service business card in Rosie's outstretched hand.

They ordered another round of pizza and beers, and soon they all left Kokopelli's full of confidence.

Chapter 5

Five-thirty a.m., Christmas eve. The store sparkled with electri-glitz decorations. Fresh spruce and evergreen scent from forest farm-cut trees awaiting their holiday homes. Supplies place neatly on shelves, computer data from last night entered, desk cleared, rubble shoveled/swept out of the construction materials zone. The hardware mega-store was lumbering toward opening time at 6 a.m.

The eastern horizon in Phoenix lingered a mottled navy. The pavement and parking lot outside glistened from a two-day drizzle. Arlen sensed more than saw the opaque outlines of remaining clouds beyond the palms and mesquite trees that separated rows of parking.

Arlen was usually the first to arrive in the morning, around 4:30 a.m., when, except for the dead of summer, the sun had not yet risen. It was quiet then, with time and space to give order to the day about to begin. He paced the rows of cut lumber, inhaling the scent of pine, redwood and cedar. He returned to the power tools and motors section, where he supervised two other guys and enforced safety regulations, ever an eye on naïve and occasionally just plain dumb machos that wanted to test the equipment before purchase.

The rows were stocked well for the busy winter season in Phoenix: power drills, power saws, battery-run drill/drivers, gas-fired chain saws, lawn mowers, Weed Eaters and hedge clippers. Electric floor cleaners and mini-cement mixers. The motor section boasted Hondas and Briggs & Strattons at 2.5 hp, 3.5 hp and one at 5 hp. He fingered the Briggs. He'd be interested in trying this one out to see if it compared to the one he had known from the daily use, daily breakdowns and years of bubblegum repairs on his family farm. It would be nice to see a brand-new one at work, dredging a stream for gold, pumping a well. He'd like to move beyond servicing the rentals that folks had abused while cleaning out garages or other parts of low-lying yards that collected rainwater after the August monsoons. While most tools did a brisk sales, motors sputtered after Thanksgiving.

Adriana, one of the checkout cashiers, stopped by with a cardboard tray of coffees. *"Café puro, amigo?"* She scraped one 16-ounce container out of the holder-tray and handed it to him. "All hogs in the barnyard?"

It was their standing joke. Both now lived here in Phoenix, working in the hardware store in Arizona, but both had been raised on farms. She in Texas, he in Iowa. They had discovered their common ground months ago: a love-hate relationship with their rural past, over chorizo burritos at Ernesto's semi permanent "Dog 'n' Taco" wagon out in front of the store.

"I like mine with lots of salsa," she had offered as an icebreaker.

Adriana was a quiet woman, appearing to be about forty-five, with a round brown face surrounded by straight black hair pulled away during working hours, a bit dumpy, as if several kids had taken their toll. Maybe that shape was genetic.

Arlen hadn't said anything to her before the burritos. You don't just casually talk to women, even fellow employees, even ones probably ten or twenty years your senior, just because you see them every day. Never know how they'll react, even if you offer a compliment.

"I do too, and sometimes I'll add extra chiles," he had

replied. "Can I offer you coffee or a soda?"

In any case, she had initiated what was turning into a comfortable "old friends" friendship. Just too much similar bad history to ignore each other. She liked his early-morning reliability at the store, and he liked that she didn't chatter on or pry too deeply.

Neither of them seemed to have a "significant other."

"You married?" he had asked.

"I was." Adriana took a slow sip of hot coffee, stared silently across the store, returned her gaze. "He was just interested in younger women. Left several years ago. Said he wasn't old enough to have a wife my age and children in their teens. As if he was some young younger version of Julio Iglesias." She chuckled. "Know him?"

Arlen had to admit he did not. Not a name that an Anglo Iowa farm boy would have casually run across.

"So, Arlen. You're young, good looking." He blushed. She was overdoing it, he thought." "Got a wife? A girlfriend?"

"No. I'm still settling into Arizona, trying to do my best here at work." Arlen didn't go into his fear of commitment, the fear of being rejected or having the tables turned. "I've got a dog, though. Stormy. He keeps me busy. Since I leave to get here at work so early in the morning, I have to spend a lot of time with him when I get home. In the winter I'll take him running on the canal or maybe to Piestewa Peak for a good workout."

"Well, I've heard that dogs are a good – as you say in English – 'chick magnet.' Don't you find that on your hikes, Arlen?"

He smiled. "Yes, but most of the buff young ladies out on the trail are with buff young men. They might stop and pet the dog, but then they run along on their way. And besides, I just don't think I'm ready yet. Let's leave it at that."

She let it go, and they stayed on safer topics: her kids, shop talk, Ernesto's family, or the weather. Being comfortable mattered to both of them much more than being too close. Adriana had figured out Arlen's modus — arriving much earlier than necessary in order to have everything clean and ready. In order to have things clean and ready for any kind of day — a call to another store, a cranky customer, lack of supplies. Just in case. That sense he'd picked up on the farm that you want to have all the animals "in the barnyard," accounted for, so to speak. No chaos greeting the day. Once the store opened, chaos would surely arrive, like Satan, in any number of disguises.

Adriana, too, liked that quiet time in the early morning. She, too, had tired of the rigors of the farm but maintained the pattern of setting the day aright early.

A cashier's tasks began at 6:00 a.m., but Adriana recognized Arlen's need to reconnoiter his zone. So she took up the modest but infectious habit of stopping by Ernesto's trailer out front. She'd arrive at the Latino's counter after brewing had begun (5:15 a.m.) but before anyone else had time to slip in front of her (5:23 a.m.). It didn't hurt that the first steaming cups of mountain-grown Chiapas coffee were also the best of the day.

She'd get Ernesto's update on his diabetic wife and difficult teenagers, a detailed report on the never-ending search for comfortable shoes, and she'd hand him a little extra tip for the early brew. She'd put four cups into a cardboard tray, set two off for the other two gals who would soon be in at the registers, and she'd go on over to Arlen's spot in machinery. She'd offer him his coffee; he'd be grateful she'd saved him the time. Then they'd spend some time, the paper cups warming their hands, sniffing the aroma of freshly ground, freshly brewed beans, and they'd gaze across the parking lot as pickups slipped into the diagonal parking slots outside. Their coffee break lasted less than ten minutes. They talked sometimes, but just as often not. It was their time for a quiet mug together.

Graduation was a much smaller affair in December than it would have been in May, but Rosie didn't want to wait. She wanted to move on. Danny came down from Flagstaff and stayed over the weekend while she divested herself of furniture and usables to friends who'd return the next semester. The crowd had been friendly, Rosie received accolades for the work she had done both in African dance and in forest analysis. She had spent almost the whole summer before her last year working, partly with Professor Pete, documenting species, growth patterns, and regeneration patterns from the forest area near the farm that had suffered a fire decades before.

The ceremony was free-spirited but at the same time intimate. Each graduating senior was introduced by one of his or her professors. Many students sported attire consistent with their chosen major. Rosie chose simply to tie her African scarf around her neck, donning the traditional cap and gown. The African dance instructor spoke with eloquence about the spirit and talent of the young lady before her.

A reception in the entrance lobby provided victuals for all graduates and their families. Health food abounded: bulgur, green salads, hot lentil soup, fresh-baked bread from the campus kitchen. Some kind soul had also remembered to provide chocolate cake as well as the "healthier" carrot cake. All appetites were satisfied. Some family had come. But the absence of Mom and Dad had hung heavily. Aunts and uncles made congratulatory remarks. Still, Rosie hung close to Danny. He knew when to be quiet and just let things be.

Danny drove back to Flag in his pickup on Sunday night with some boxes, and Rosie followed on Tuesday in the Jeep Cherokee with the rest of her belongings.

Christmas broke cold and clear on Saturday. Danny's friends brought various dishes and Danny manned the charcoal cooker, smoking a turkey and grilling a slab of barbecued salmon. Rosie gave him a set of chest-high waders for dredge work. Danny gave her two compact emergency power lights, with a night-light, flare light, compass, radio and siren all combined in a slender column. It was, thought Rosie, as if Danny already knew her plan.

The last friend left about 11 p.m., and Danny's roommates either were out of state or with girlfriends. They threw a few more logs in the fireplace, settled the dogs, and sipped some holiday wine. Danny had decided to savor the bouquet of the sauvignon. He swirled each sip around on his tongue before swallowing.

Rosie tried the same, and found the aroma – the bouquet – more pronounced than with a mere gulp. She read the label and chuckled. "Does this one really have a 'fruity bouquet and a touch of woody musk with a smooth finish'? I swear, there's a whole industry just in describing wines." They laughed easily at the pretentiousness on the back of the bottle. Then Rosie posed the idea.

"Danny, why don't we start a farm up at Clear Creek? I talked to a bunch of friends in Prescott and there are a couple of us who could live there full time. We could terrace the field, pipe in some irrigation to water crops, fix up the chicken coop, and sell eggs and veggies at Farmers Market all summer. I could harvest herbs for salves and tinctures. You could come weekends. What do you think, Danny? I know it's cold right now, but I think we could make a go of it starting in a few months."

She presented it like a business plan. She and some of the folks around the college would live at the ranch house. It had once been a deeded base camp of a ranch deep within the National Forest. It had a few bedrooms, a loft, and a wide covered porch that circled three sides. There was plenty of room for regulars and occasional visitors to make Clear Creek Farm a respected entity in the Yavapai community.

Never you mind that it was off the grid, isolated in the mountains, accessible only by 4WD, and there was no farming community within miles. She, Sam, Tony and Arielle could do it. Chris might join them. Pete could offer his connections with the college. Chloe had experience with the Yavapai Extension Service of the University of Arizona School of Agriculture. She served all sorts of farming, gardening, forestry and animal hudbandry needs in Yavapai County, from the open farms of Chino Valley to the Prescott National Forest. The others were wrapping up or had dropped out of college with courses in sustainable farming or some such, they would pool their funds, live low on the food chain, and sustain themselves.

"But, Rosie, what would keep you going until you made money? And you've never been a real farmer. And who are these guys? Do you really know them? Honest, it seems so far-fetched …"

"Brother of mine, I'm sure it could work. Three of us have solid construction or farming experience. The land is free for the using. We can live in the ranch house. In the summer we'll sleep on the veranda. I could use a little of the trust fund. Just the cost of some construction materials and some fencing, and then seeds, and we can get the whole project going."

Danny poked a log to stir up some embers, tossed another log on, and leaned back in the rug-covered armchair. Sipped more sauvignon to stall. Even though he felt the idea couldn't exactly fly, he was only two years older. It didn't feel quite right to nix her plan. She'd have friends around, they'd be working on an interesting project, there would be food grow-ing, the already-fallen trees could be cut for firewood, and he could check in while dredging every weekend or so.

"Tell ya what, Sis, let's go to the farm for New Year's week-end. It'll be cold, but there's no forecast for snow. We should be able to drive in and out safely. We can walk the property and get a better feel for how a few people could live in the house and make things work."

"I knew you'd see the brilliance of my plan," Rosie said happily. "Let's drink to that. I love the idea of spending that stupid holiday out in the woods, away from drunken revelers. Do you want to bring the dogs?"

Danny paused. He hadn't told her before now, but two of his roommates were bailing out, planning to leave their pets behind. Feeding them all, cleaning up after them, and getting them exercise was a significant daily commitment. The casualness with which college students traded dogs out like used books offended him. He had grown deeply attached to Shepherd pup. He loved the Lab and the Pitt Bull too. He knew he could not let them go to complete strangers.

"We have a situation with the dogs. Two of my roommates are moving, either in with a girlfriend or back east, and they don't want to keep their dogs. Willie here," he patted the Shepherd pup, "well, he's mine. But the other two, Brutus and Bella, they need a new home."

"What if they come live at the farm with me? I know them already. I've been here a bunch, and I've been helping out taking care of them the last few days. They know me. I'd love to have them."

Daniel mulled that one over. Dogs have a new home, Rosie has some watchdogs. While it was generally safe up at the farm, you never knew. It seemed like a good idea.

"Let's take them with us," he suggested. "If we go in the Cherokee all three dogs can fit in, and we'll see how they like it."

Monday Rosie shopped for food and supplies. Danny made calls to the roommates about Brutus and Bella. Replies were favorable. They both spent time online researching placer mining, homesteading, and farming at the Prescott altitude. By Thursday evening they were ready.

After treating Rosie to one of his specialties, a Thai green curry dinner, Danny lit another fire and proffered some chamomile tea.

"Rosie, there's something we haven't talked about. Something we haven't done."

The room sombered. Rosie's jaw tensed. Her eyes fixed upon the embers. "I know."

"Mom and Dad. Their ashes. We never did anything. I put their urns in my closet. Couldn't stand the mantelpiece."

"So...you think... now?"

"Yeah. On the hill above the meadow. They'd walk there together. Her brother is there."

"I don't know if I'm ready."

"Tell ya what. Let's take the urns, and if we feel right about it, we'll do it."

They packed Friday morning, tanked up and bought a good supply of comfort food – aka "junk" — at the Kachina Convenience Mart where Hotchkiss worked, west of Milton on Route 66. They left early Friday afternoon, arriving in time to light a serious fire both in the fireplace and the wood-burning stove. They brought enough wood inside so that whoever woke in the night could stoke the fires.

The road to the farm wove through jagged mountains, first of high chaparral, prickly pear cactus and juniper, then rising in elevation among ponderosa and spruce. The countryside appeared dry and forbidding, even with a light layer of snow dusting the angulated hillsides. As they approached the farm, folds of mountains parted, opening upon several cleared acres that ascended gradually on either side of a sinuous dark creek toward a line of trees bordering the meadow that was to become their terraced garden.

The farmhouse, a compact log building supporting a corrugated tin roof, stood carved out of a slope facing the creek and a view that extended across to the expansive open meadow. It had been built in the 1930s when some homesteaders gained title to both a mining claim and deeded land, carved out of the Prescott National Forest at a time when Federal policy supported mining and ranching in the West. The property had served several prior owners; first as a homesteading farm; next as respite for an alcoholic baseball has-been; then as the base camp for a cattle ranch; and finally, for Mom and Dad, as a retreat from city life.

Currently a local rancher still ran cattle through the property. There was ease and cooperation among the forest users, an understanding that no one would overstep their privileges and easements, and everyone would watch out for each other and for the forest itself. Hunters scoped out hunting grounds all year round, but they hunted only with licenses and in season. There was a code of respect for the numbers allotted by Arizona Fish and Game. Bow hunters and gun hunters had their own months in which to hunt separately, primarily as a safety provision for the humans.

Inside, the kitchen housed a large wood-burning stove. A massive fireplace, built of Bradshaw granite, dominated the living/dining room. A seat-high hearth hosted a stock of logs and kindling. Windows on all sides exposed a view of meadow and mountainside and the occasional birds that visited trees closest to the house.

The farm was almost off the grid. That meant no electricity, cell phone only from the driveway, and no TV. The farm did have an indoor toilet that Dad had rigged up by piping a PVC line up the hill from the well to an old water tank, and then letting gravity bring it to the house for a kitchen sink and a flush toilet. From there everything flowed out to a large evapo-transmission bed, aka septic tank. The luxury of an indoor toilet was much appreciated when the thermometer on the porch read below freezing.

From the farm house, a stand of young pines rose in the southwest, all born the same year from the heat and ashes of a fire that had swept perilously close to the farm house but left the building and acreage almost untouched. Beyond the saplings rose a ridge of green, living ponderosa, mixed among burned trunks — remains awaiting a harsh wind and the inevitable crash to the forest floor. Beyond the ridge other mountains receded in dusty azure, lavender, and violet, south toward Bumble Bee and Crown King. This stark beautiful land was not cut out for easy farming.

To the northwest rose a massive peak, beyond which yet higher peaks were known, but not visible. The only view Rosie and Danny could see from the farmhouse was the meadow, the hills covered with Ponderosa and deciduous trees, then the distant mountainside. Here, in winter, the dark twisted branches of oak and walnut stood out distinctly against the light snow blanketing dead leaves. A few spruce coned upward, their short, needled branches in silvery blue jostling against nearby dark greens of the long-needled pines.

Near the creek, a mix of oak, walnut, alder and cottonwood drank from deep underground waters. A row of apple trees, planted by the first homesteader, framed the edge of the creek, nakedly awaiting spring's buds and blossoms.

On Saturday morning Rosie and Danny hiked the perimeter of the property boundaries. Upstream, there were posts for fencing that ran up the steep, rocky hillsides and around the stand of new pines above the meadow. They followed that line and saw numerous tracks of deer, coyote, squirrel and rabbit. Danny wasn't sure if some other tracks indicated bear or mountain lion. They were known to be in the forest but were both elusive, avoiding exposure to humans. Thinking of Rosie at the farm, possibly alone, he hoped not.

Descending on the far southwestern side of the field, they again crossed the creek and inspected the well. Hand-dug and built in the 1930s, it still served to deliver an ample supply of water for the house and a small garden. A larger field this summer would test its capacity. They struggled to start up the pump. Danny finally succeeded in getting a prime, and they waited for a while as water surged through the underground PVC line uphill to the tank.

The pump had faltered several previous times. It was taking longer to spark into action. The pull-cord was proving too long and too difficult for Rosie alone. It had always seemed so easy when Dad pulled the starter. Danny was taller than Dad. His height and long legs and arms provided a greater stretch. He could pull the cord all the way out, while Rosie couldn't. But, for today, everything was ok. The pump reached its full pressure quickly. Rosie sighed, relieved.

"Looks like the well is in good shape." Danny removed the metal top and watched the level recede as the water hose poured the well's contents into an underground line that led uphill to the storage tank. "We might have to lower ourselves into the well during the warm weather and scoop out some accumulated mud from the bottom."

"We can do that." Rosie thought it might actually be a fun way to cool off while getting a job done. She replaced the metal cover, sliding it over the cement edge. Danny cut the motor.

They walked up the hill to inspect the chicken coop. It needed new posts, reinforced fencing and new doors for the hens to enter and exit. But the roosting beams were all in place and the roof had no leaks. It was a manageable project.

By dinnertime Rosie had won Danny over. At best, they could work a sustainable farm. At the very least, a bunch of people could guard the place and fix it up a bit, and Danny could check in with Rosie every weekend or two to make sure things were going okay. It would be simple to pull the plug on the operation in short order — just move the livestock and call it quits.

They awoke on Sunday morning to a bowl of ice on the porch that had been drinking water for the dogs. Frost edged the windowpanes. The thermometer on a post read 20 degrees Fahrenheit. They brewed a strong pot of percolated coffee on the wood-burner and Rosie served up a stack of buckwheats and maple syrup to complement Danny's sizzled bacon.

It was on both their minds. Rosie didn't want to talk about it, but she knew they had to. They both took extra time savoring breakfast and lingering over a second cup of coffee. It was easy to linger: the view out the large picture window by the dining room table was framed with two tall ponderosa and the creek flowing below, black and busy against the snowy banks and jutting rocks. They watched the gushing stream and wisps of dry sere grass, poking out of the snow and waving slightly in the morning breeze. A Western Jay, blue with a black crest, darted from one tree to the other, seeking sustenance in the cold.

Danny started. "This morning a good time?"

"Yes." Rosie knew.

"The hill beyond the meadow?"

"But let's scatter them in among the pines and junipers, not exposed in the open meadow, ok?"

After cleaning up, they laced their boots, added gloves and scarves against the winter chill, and carried the urns up past the old stone wall to a leveled off opening.

"Danny, I can't think of any prayers they'd like."

"It's ok, Sis. We did enough of prayers and songs at the memorial service. Just being here, they'll be at peace. This is their place."

Rosie studied the urn in her heavy gloves. She stared out across the slope. She placed it on the ground. "Danny,

I haven't really told you, but I'm still angry at them. They should have protected me. I miss them, and I'm mad at them. It hurts, Danny, it hurts."

Danny set down his urn. He bundled his little sister against his huge parka and stood with her a long while, just feeling the stiffness, then the sobs, then the release of tension and the calm. He had no words of comfort, no solutions. Not for her, not for him. Just sadness.

A limb on the far hillside cracked and fell into the nearest juniper. It didn't hit ground, just remained suspended in the winter tangle of boughs and branches. Unfinished, like the business of life, the business of loss.

Rosie finally disentangled herself. They looked briefly at each other. Then, each one took an urn and carefully removed the lid. Together, the let fall their parents' ashes, mingling, catching slightly in the breeze, until every bit had fallen into the light snow cover and nestled among oak leaves and pine needles. They stood silently for a few moments. Then, silently, they walked together back down the hill.

Barking at possible rabbits and bounding through a swirling section of icy water, the dogs caught up to them as they reached the stream.

Danny and Rosie packed silently. Finally, Rosie tugged them both away from their deep sadness to a space more hopeful.

"Thanks for walking the property with me, Danny, and checking out the well. Do you still feel ok about the sustainable farm?"

"Sure, Sis. I think you can do it, and I'll help however I can. I will find a big gold nugget, you can be sure of that!"

"Danny, what makes you think I'm not looking for gold too?" Rosie opened the back door of the Cherokee and let the dogs hop in and settle themselves around the cooler and blankets.

Danny opened the driver's side and climbed in. He motioned for her to climb in so they could get going. "Sis, if there's one thing I know, it's that if you set your heart on something, you'll get it done. If it's gold you're looking for, and there is gold in Clear Creek, sure as shooting you will find gold. I can't think of anyone — besides me, of course — who deserves to find gold more than you. Here's wishing us both a pot at the end of the rainbow."

"But for a day job, the farm is a good idea too."

Rosie climbed in on the right side of the Jeep, put an extra thermos of coffee in the car's center holder, and sighed.

It looked like it was going to happen.

Chapter 6

Gigantic strings of Valentine hearts and smiley bears dangled optimistically between the rows of plumbing, hardware, lumber and motors. Arlen had weathered the Christmas season a little lonely but doing well in sales. The store kept busy with seasonal décor, presumably to cheer the workforce and entice customers to do more impulse buying. The sky was lightening a little earlier than it had in December and the days were moving steadily toward the spring equinox, a balance of night and day, when it was easier to sustain a positive outlook and get some good evening hikes in with his dog. He started to daydream a little about where he might want to explore in this big, diverse southwestern state.

"Excuse me, do you work here?" A clear voice, soft yet strong, came from behind.

Arlen had been replacing equipment from the stockroom after a run on battery-run drill/drivers. He turned to see blue eyes as clear as a mountain-fed stream picking up on the ID label on his jacket.

Yes, he worked there. His job was to help her.

"What can I do for you?" He tried not to stare. Short, maybe even petite, in hip-cut jeans and a blue plaid flannel shirt over a tank top, the shirt's blue resonating with those eyes. Hiking boots quite scuffed, but a bundle of soft dark curls pushed behind a bandana that showed the colors of a copper sun and the stunning red and gold stripes of sunrise in Arizona fanning out around. Usually the customers were guys in work overalls, smudged with drying cement mix or paint, looking for a new power drill or chain saw, or with a part or a tool in hand. Or they were ladies here in the store on orders from a husband, women who weren't too sure what to make of heavy machinery.

She was clearly not part of a construction crew. She didn't look like she could handle heavy lifting. Yet there was something rather concrete about the way she directed her question, as if she were quite able to tell a Phillips from an Allen wrench, and that if Arlen presumed ignorance he would be delivering an insult. "This is power tools and motors, right?" She looked around the shelves and at some heavy machinery sitting on the floor.

Correct.

"You're in the right place, if that's what you're looking for. What is it in particular I can help you with?"

Lord, her eyes were lovely.

"Long story, but I'll try to make it short." He was surprisingly comfortable to talk to, this slightly chunky fellow with what appeared to be calluses on his hands. "I live on this farm in the Prescott National Forest area. We're off the grid, and we have a creek that runs by, and a well. We pump the water from the well up to a water tank uphill from the house. Well, that's not quite right. We pump some of it up to the water tank, but we also have the capacity to divert it to another line and pump it across the creek for irrigating a field of vegetables. There's a T in the PVC pipe where we can change the direction of the flow when we're watering crops. We're doing a start-up sustainable farm."

"Wow, that sounds like pretty hard work." Arlen had to admire her ambition and her plumbing knowledge. It was a pretty safe bet that she wasn't local. Coming down from the Prescott area. Maybe she had local ties. "So how can I help?"

"Well," Rosie hesitated. She didn't want to admit that the pump was giving her problems. "I've been having a hard time building pressure in our water pump at the well. I wondered if there was something wrong with the ignition or the fuel mix, and what part I might need to replace to get it running better."

"What kind of a pump do you have?" Arlen led her away from table saws and circular saws toward motors, pumps in particular.

"It's a Briggs & Stratton 3.5 horsepower."

"That's a pretty solid piece of equipment."

She clearly knew her motor. How pleasant dealing with someone who knew her stuff, *and* who wasn't a guy. She seemed knowledgeable but maybe not as presumptuous. Maybe readier to ask the necessary questions. And pretty. A definite benefit.

"So how long've you had it? It should work pretty well." Good piece of equipment, he thought. It shouldn't lose its power.

"We've had it …" Rosie caught her breath. She thought about the dozens of times she and Dad had worked on the pump. Dad had been able to start it after several hefty pulls on the cord. Then they had watched together as the needle hovered around 8-10 pounds, climbed slowly to 15, then to over 35 psi, and they'd know the water was pumping up the hill to the tank they had brought in over 15 years ago. That was when she was just a kid, when they all came as a family …so very long ago. Now, Dad would never be there again to help. She was on her own. There was no more "we." But it had worked so well when Dad had started it.

"It's been in the family for quite some time," she finally volunteered. "Probably 15 years or more. I was a kid when we got it. We just used it to pump water up the hill to the tank above the house. We never used it for irrigating terraced vegetables. Maybe it's too much to ask."

Why were her eyes misting? Had he done anything wrong? Clearly there was some history to this motor that she hadn't divulged, that was vital to her need to make this Briggs & Stratton stay in working order. Sentimentality? Not something you can really afford when the job needs doing. Usually not the feeling one had for a pump. He'd stay in tune for another clue.

"That shouldn't be a problem," he offered. "Here's the deal. You know it's done the job to get water to the tank for the house. Is the field where you water the crops at a higher elevation? That could affect the pump's capacity."

"No, it's lower. There's a little bit longer line of PVC, but the grade is lower. So I don't get it." She was back to business now, her brow no longer furrowed, no tears about to brim over. Good.

"Well, you've got it right then. Elevation should be the determining factor. So have you any theories of what might be causing the problem? I mean, is there really a problem?"

"Well, of course there's a problem or I wouldn't be here," Rosie snapped. Was he taking her for a dummy? But then, she didn't want to admit even to herself there was a problem, so why give the guy grief when he was trying to help?

Rosie checked herself. She'd done this before, snap at a guy just because he asked a question. As if he would hurt her and she had to defend herself. She'd turned off more guys on simple questions than she could count. It seemed to come from somewhere in the past, somewhere dark, somewhere that had no relationship to the question or the person. It was the same here. A simple question, and a huge reaction. She'd have to figure this out. It put people on guard for the wrong reasons, and she didn't like herself for it.

She lightened up. "Sorry. I mean, yes, there is a problem, and I'm not sure what it is. I can get it started, but it takes so many more pulls of the damn cord than it ever took Dad or Danny. But Danny — he's my brother," she quickly added, — "isn't always around. He lives in Flagstaff. So it's between me and Sam to get the job done. And, frankly, Sam doesn't have a gift with motors. Give him a gun. Put him with the chickens. Those are his strong suits. Same with Tony. And Arielle, well, she's sweet but …"

Wondering who Sam, Tony and Arielle were in the equation, Arlen waited.

"Oh, I got off the point, didn't I?" She gave a little laugh, sort of self-deprecating, acknowledging that she'd wandered far afield from the motor. "Sorry about that." Eyes clear again. "Sam is one of my business partners. Plus, there's Tony and Arielle. Sam knows chicken farming. Tony knows construction. I've got the farm. I know plants; I know the motor pretty well. We're all learning the business. But this is still off the point."

Thank goodness this was a slow day. This gal appealed to him: her slender build, her strong blue eyes and dark curly hair. Her clear complexion and softly rounded cheekbones. And her story intrigued him. He, too, knew farms, though he was glad not to have the responsibility of one–and he knew a lot about equipment.

"So, let me get this. Is it just the four of you? And how close to town are you? You mentioned that you're in the mountains, which doesn't sound much like farming country. How'd that all come to pass?"

They were no longer looking at motor parts, but she didn't look directly at him either. Maybe personal stuff had come up too quickly. But she did seem to want to keep talking, for now. Unclear whether it would solve the mystery of how to work, or fix, or adjust the pump.

"By the way, I'm Arlen." He stuck out his hand. She had a firm grip. Her smile, a little crooked, revealed even white teeth and naturally pink lips. Her soft round cheeks were flushed with sunshine. He wondered if she was aware how pretty she was, how enchanting her smile.

"Rosie. Nice to meet you." His hand was big, rough and warm. He seemed genuinely interested but did not invade her space. A gentleman, perhaps.

"You know, Rosie," Arlen mused, "I grew up on a farm. We had a lot of heavy equipment, including a Briggs & Stratton. We pumped water from a nearby stream to a tank for the cattle out in the field. It would be a lot easier if I could see what you're talking about. Any way you could bring in the whole thing? Is it locked in place?"

"No, we sit it on a flat rock and haul it back to the storage shed when it rains. Which isn't that often. But it has spent some nights out in the weather. So it could have suffered a bit from the rain and snow." She paused. "Where are you from? The Southwest, where it doesn't rain so much? Or somewhere else? I don't mean to be a regionalist but it's pretty different here in Arizona."

"You're right, it is. Iowa farm. Rain was more regular. But we'd have our dry spells too."

Iowa farm boy. Big calloused hands. No ring on ring finger, though that wasn't conclusive in guys. Hadn't hit on her. Despite her reservations about guys in general, despite a vague anxiety about any and all dating, she found him interesting and attractive. More than that, he felt safe. Maybe it was the softness, like her brother Danny. Danny exuded trustworthiness. He wouldn't hurt a fly, much less a woman. After living together in the "haunted house" that fall, after sharing their ugliest fears and sorrows, Rosie had found Danny to be boundlessly honorable. It was as if he had an aura – that you could tell from his very presence – that you were safe.

This Mister Arlen guy seemed the same. Perhaps it was that he appeared to have worked hard on a farm. Like maybe he had been hurt or known sorrow. But instinctively she felt that he would not harm her. Where that came from, she couldn't explain. But there was something even in the handshake. A leap of faith took even Rosie by surprise.

"What if we did it the other way around?" she asked. "Why don't you come up this weekend and take a look at the thing on-site? Then you'll understand exactly how the system works. Maybe you can make suggestions."

"Wow." Hadn't seen that one coming. A come-on? Didn't feel like one. "Well, yes. Maybe yes." He felt himself short of clever words and phrases to sound more interested or grateful. He realized that she picked up on his hesitation.

"It's a pretty spot, Mr. Arlen. C'mon. It's a nice little ranch house by a creek surrounded by oak, walnut and pine. Really a great getaway from Phoenix. It does sometimes take a 4X4. You got a truck and a sleeping bag? Sam has cornered most of the extra blankets. It gets cool at nights. The dogs and I pretty much take over the main bedroom." *There, I'm establishing some boundaries. It's clear, isn't it?*

Arlen mulled it over, but quickly. "I have a Ford F-150, and it's 4WD, so I'm set with a truck. Got a working GPS, so if you have a map and general directions, I should be able to get there. Got a sleeping bag, and, if I need it, a tent and general camping equipment — stove, tarp, stuff like that. But I have…" He paused. The next question was sometimes a stopper. "I have a dog. Stormy. I pretty much don't go anywhere without him. Is that ok?"

"That should be easy. I've got two. If they can figure out how to get along there shouldn't be a problem. And it's the woods for heaven's sake. They can romp around and chase rabbits." Rosie smiled. The notion of the dogs chasing around in the forest brought an inward smile, and another reason to believe there were diversions enough to fend off trouble. She relaxed.

"I'll bring a bunch of tools and supplies for what the pump might need." Arlen gave her his business card. "But the next few weekends are kind of busy for me. How would early- to mid-March do?"

"Fine. I can call you or text. We don't get Internet at the farm. I sometimes go into Prescott and use my laptop, so …" She looked at the card. "Is this a good e-mail?"

"Yup."

"Well, that'll be right fine, then. Maybe you'll be more help than either of us expected."

"Hope so." Arlen smiled back He caught another glimpse of her crooked little smile. He shouldn't take so much notice, but it was hard not to. "Let's be in touch soon. And thanks for coming in."

"*Au contraire*. The pleasure was mine."

Rosie put his business card in her purse, walked past the checkout counters, and exited the automatic doors. Arlen watched her shirt sway with each step and cling to her hips until some trucks drove through customer pick-up and cut her out of his line of sight.

Well, that seemed like a pleasant chat." Adriana had come over on her lunch break. "Who was the lovely young lady?"

"Rosie. I mean, well, um, she introduced herself. She has a problem with a motor. She lives on a farm in the mountains outside Prescott."

Adriana offered him a small dish of corn chips and a cup of salsa. "Want me to get you a Coke?"

"Sure."

She returned from the soda machine with a can in each hand. "Well, she seemed pretty attentive."

Arlen demurred. "She is pretty, I'll say that. Nice change from the construction crew regulars. But that's all."

Adriana popped to top off her Coke, took a fizzy sip. "I'll be on the lookout."

Chapter 7

He heard about the crash quite by accident. He was tending bar on the west side now, miles away from where the parents and the two kids had lived. Didn't read the papers, didn't drive that way. The injunction sealed that off. He wasn't fool enough to toy with the police any more than he had already. He'd stopped most of his drinking, he'd stopped speeding, and no, he had no way of asking the family for anything. They'd have called the cops.

So, when Casey dropped by the bar one night a year and a half ago, it had been a surprise — the news — not Casey being at the bar, he'd become a regular. They both liked the occasional game of pool, talk about sports, and maybe hitting on some chick who'd come to the Club Deportiva alone.

He and Casey went way back. The two of them had ditched high school and burglarized each other's neighborhoods, back when he still lived with the family. It was humiliating when something he stole from a car on Casey's street, miles away, turned out to have a name in the briefcase that belonged to some friend of theirs. And by then the parents were at least smart enough to wait until he fell asleep at dawn before they brought in the cops. Cuffed and taken straight to juvenile detention.

Funny they had never caught on to what went down with the girl. Not for the longest time. Not until after he had moved out and she had moved out and finally ratted on him. No longer afraid of his threat to kill her and her brother if she told. They were clueless about the times they went out for just a short time, maybe to the gym or getting groceries, when he could get her in her bedroom, muffle her sounds, getting it off while using his hands to molest and terrorize her.

Jeez, her body had been so little. Hard to remember it now that he sought women his own age. Anglo, Hispanic, he didn't care. Not interested in Black women. Wanted to stick closer to his own kind. But her little flat breast had been so – so white, compared to his own dark skin. Just a little girl. Wonder he remembered at all. It was so unimportant.

He'd never thought of them as being sister and brother anyway. *They* looked like each other. *He* looked different. He had his own memories of his real mother, his early childhood. Enough so he didn't want to accept that he was placed with a new family after his own father went to prison and his mom was murdered. So angry at his own parents for abandoning him. Angry at having to accept a totally new situation. Wanting a way to take out his anger on someone. So taking it out on her was easy.

But they were both kids, weren't they? So what if he was six years older? Girls wanted it. When he had lived in foster care, everyone did it. An older girl had hit on him and it felt good. Actually, not all that good. There was that nagging apprehension he felt about having something stolen from him. But he was a guy, macho. He did jack off with this teen girl, even if he was only seven or eight. Jeez, it was unsettling. He had just been fooling around in the yard with the animals when she had taken him into the barn, away from what he thought he wanted to do. Made him play with her and with himself. Then they'd come back there a coupla times more. It was a hiding place, away from the foster mother, who was usually busy cooking for everyone. She never noticed. He'd do it with this older girl, and it was sort of exciting. Why did remembering it put a pit in his stomach? Didn't he really like it? Didn't all guys like it? Anytime? That was what all the kids said in the boys' locker room. That was sure what he had tried to accomplish once puberty hit. Lots of girls, lots of cunts, lots of sex. He proved that he was a man – every time.

Anyway, after all those years, when she finally told her parents, they cut him off. From the car, the house, the money. He'd tried to wait until they cooled down and slide back into normalcy, but they slapped a court injunction on him, against any contact in any form, at work or schools or house, even e-mails.

So he'd moved to the west side. The DUIs had resulted in no driver's license for a year, so his job choices were limited for a while. Had to find a job within walking distance. Had to live with roommates. What a joke. If you wanted to get away from guys who drank too much, living with roommates on the west side was not the way to do it.

Now he had his own place, close to the bar. He still lived within walking distance, but the Deportiva was a pretty good bar. A sports bar. He'd been competitive in some sports and voraciously devoured news on anything athletic. Any athlete who came on the screen — well, he knew their stats and could chew the fat with the guys at the counter. Moreover, somewhere along the line, he'd picked up some skills at diverting the aggression sometimes associated with drinking and sports betting. Not quite sure where this skill came from, considering how he had treated her and her brother. It hadn't fit with the girls and women he had dated along the line. There'd been three Orders of Protection against him from old girlfriends.

So maybe that was where it came from. Getting to a point where you absolutely couldn't lash out or the cops would have you prone on the ground with your hands cuffed behind you, spending a night in jail. Although it didn't have enough of an effect on how he handled the women he slept with, on his come-from-nowhere angry outbursts, it did turn his mind toward the notion of using his smarts to outsmart the men whose alcohol intake made them think they could assault anyone — man or woman — inside the Club Deportiva.

Now the only time he really felt any anger anymore was against women. Not all women. Just his mother, for abandoning him by dying in a bar fight. And now, just the ones that got too close. Not every woman he slept with. There were enough of them who were just useful for casual sex. It was just the women who started expecting a relationship. Anyone who pried a layer off his shell.

So, in the Club Deportiva — this bar had a little pretense that amused him — his steely calm came in handy. The boss liked it. Often asked him to step around the counter and help someone get a grip or go outside.

Well, that was then, this was now. He'd stopped being connected to the parents after the injunction. Still, when Casey showed him the headline — "Couple killed in highway pileup" — it was a surprise.

Ever since arriving, straight from foster care, into their family to become adopted, they had been there for him as real parents. The mother got him into school, then special classes for his hyper vigilance. He didn't seem to be able to let go of the nightmares of his early childhood. She rushed to the school nurse when he had panic attacks. She never guessed his panic surrounded what he had just done to their daughter, and the fear he would be caught.

The father helped him with math, cheered at every baseball game, every track meet statewide. They helped carpool, they chaperoned, they praised him. When he won and offered support when he came in second. He would *never* let himself come in less than second. They helped him get a driver's license. They went with him every time to juvenile court. They took him to family counseling. They got him a car, even loaned him their old one when he managed to wreck the first one. Kindly, clueless, caring, generous and without boundaries. He had counted on them. They, he thought, even loved him.

That was the part that was so hard to believe. A birth father who had gone to prison, a mother who abandoned him for drugs, foster parents who took him in for money, and here was this couple who did everything that added up to love. And he had done nasty stuff with their daughter and beat up her brother –many times. More times than he could remember. He never felt they were his brother and sister. Why treat them like they were?

He pursed his lips, looked away. Then back to Casey.

"Any more information? A funeral? The kids still in town?"

"No other news. The kids in town not very likely."

Seemed the brother was headed for Flagstaff. And when Casey had last heard, there was something about her moving to California. Remembered something about relatives in San Francisco.

She was hardheaded, as he recalled, a fearsome opponent once they were both older. But at least she'd kept her mouth shut until after high school. Since all they did was an injunction and no criminal complaint, he wagered she'd gotten pissed with them and left. Well, good. The town felt less ominous with her out of town. Better yet, out of state.

He and Casey had chewed the fat about the D-Backs and Cards, and Casey took up with a few other guys he knew and headed off to the pool tables. They had exchanged casual remarks about the women hanging around the bar that night and then split.

Despite a major win onscreen in the playoffs, a shadowy depression had pervaded the rest of the August evening, and he couldn't bring himself to joke around with the patrons. He had left right after closing and slept late into the next day.

Chapter 8

When the Prescott crowd sorted themselves out, only four decided to give it a go. Sam, who had worked on a couple of farms in California, was in. Good, he sounded like he had real experience. Tony and Arielle voted in, since they wanted to do farming. This looked good. Arielle cheered Rosie just by being around, bringing her music.

Chris, the guy Rosie had been drawn to, had decided not to move out to the farm with everyone, but instead to come visit and help with work on the weekends. His job in Prescott paid the bills, and he had to support an aging dad. Some inner clock of erotica told him this wasn't a good move. He liked Rosie. Really liked her. She was cute, she was spunky. But there was something about her that put him off – a kind of sexual unavailability. He'd love to go to bed with her – she was a hottie – but she didn't seem like the kind who could have a friendly affair and break it off if either one of them found another romance.

There were too many cute women at the college and hanging around in town to want to sleep with just one. So, rather than be in residence out at the farm and maybe getting into an emotional mess, he pulled back. He'd hate to be living there, get something going with her, change his mind and be stuck. Wouldn't be fair to either of them. Especially her. She'd grow to need him. Girls did that – get attached. And she'd really need him for the farm. So, weekends would have to do. If it developed into something more, fine. But not now.

Rosie alternated her weeks between the Phoenix hardware store, staying with Ari and Tony in Prescott, and visiting Danny in Flagstaff. It hadn't snowed much, so she and Danny went to Clear Creek farm twice during February and laid the dredge inside a hollowed-out elbow in the creek where some dislodged, broken-off tree trunks had been jammed.

Placer mining, especially for gold, opened every creek and river in the Bradshaw Mountains during the 19th and early 20th centuries. The Bradshaws were the highest and steepest range in what became the Prescott National Forest. Under the United States Mining Act of 1872, prospectors of all stripes searched every mountain cranny for gold. Many claims were staked along virtually every creek, where the sharp descent of tributaries down mountain crevasses increased the chance of exposing a new vein.

The twists and turns in the creek were most likely to expose a new lode or some chips or nuggets. As water cascaded down the steep folds of hillsides into the creek, the sheer force of the stream might erode the banks and allow undiscovered minerals to surface. As water rounded a bend, gold — the heaviest substance, either rock or metal — was less likely to shoot around the bend and flow in the coursing spring run-off from winter snows.

At the farm, several nooks and crooks had collected debris. Rosie and Danny targeted a hollow slightly upstream. An old maple, roots increasingly exposed as the soil of the river bank eroded, finally fell, crashing into logs and splinters against the rocks. They held together in a logjam.

Brother and sister hauled all the logs out of the clogged stream and water flowed through swiftly. A new lode might just expose itself. Ever on the fantasy quest for gold, Danny donned the new boots. He placed the sump pump on a flat rock and laid out the suction hose into a little upstream pool, under water. He set out the other hoses into the pool they had created by the log removal and set the sluice box and 4-inch dredge a little further downstream. He pulled the cord.

The motor started up quickly. He grabbed the handle of the vacuum hose and steered it around the bottom and sides of the pool, much like Mom had done with a vacuum cleaner on the living room carpet at home. Within seconds, gravelly water poured into and across the sluice box.

On the last weekend in February, Danny was sure he had a few flecks. He put them in a small pillbox in his pocket. "Gonna be a rich man, little sister. We's gonna find a real strain of gold in this here crik."

They hiked the entire perimeter of their acreage, going up washes and over ridges, then back down and across the meadow and creek, up behind the chicken coop and around back to the farmhouse. They surveyed the farm together, ran some barbed wire where the old property fencing had collapsed, posted some "No Trespassing" signs, and staked out the field.

"You'll need a lot of help," Danny said, surveying the uneven, grassy, rock-studded meadow. "You sure four of you can do it?"

"Sure we can. We have a lot of friends who said they'd be out here a lot to help. We'll host barbecues. It'll be work, and fun. Can't you just feel it?" Rosie swept her arms around as if they were the magic wands that would bring it instantly into being. "Danny, it's still cold now, but in a few weeks it will start to thaw. Wait until you see the progress we'll make by May."

Arlen rustled around in the garage for the equipment that would cover a lot of possibilities at this Clear Creek farm outing. Stormy, his shorthaired mutt, snooped around the shelves for loose kibbles.

First, he rounded up camping gear: sleeping bag and inflatable cushion; tent (just in case); camping stove; a box of hooks, utensils, ropes and ties; matches; extra canister of fuel; a tarp; shovel; Coleman lamp; odds and ends in plastic packets from other trips.

Next, he popped open the lid to the dog-food bin and scooped out a supply that could last beyond the weekend. Just in case. Put the food in another, smaller lidded container and added it to the "farm" stack building up on the garage floor. The King Cab stood in the driveway, waiting for just such an adventure. It was built for off-road, and the last trip they'd taken was too long ago. In good weather Arlen could throw everything into the bed of the truck. Stormy would jump into the front seat. There was room for a canine in the back seat if one might happen along. If it rained, they could store most of the gear.

So far there hadn't been a lot of human company. Now in his late twenties, Arlen had not even come close to finding 'the right girl.' He couldn't exactly put his finger on what about the farm in Iowa had turned him against commitment. Maybe it was the lackluster relationship between his parents, who just seemed to hang on for lack of a better option. There never seemed to be a spark between them.

More likely it had been the way the family settled who would inherit and take charge of the farm. Even though he had gone to school in town and had not thought of himself as continuing a rural farm life, he had always done his share of work at home. He had focused mainly on the equipment and kept everything in working order. He had learned a fair amount of animal husbandry. Nothing anyone ever had cause to complain about.

But one day, a few years ago, Dad had said the entire place was going to his brother. No questions to ask, that's just the way it was going to be. His brother had said he wanted to stay there and work the farm and take over when Dad couldn't do it any more. Arlen wasn't welcome to stay. "Better find a different line of work, son."

So he'd left, feeling a sharp betrayal by his family. He decided not to look back, and came to Phoenix, where he landed a job at the hardware store.

"In case you missed any," he said, cupping some kibbles for the eager nose that wasted no time in scarfing them down.

He ruffled Stormy's head and stubbly-furred shoulders. The physical wounds had healed well, and except for a slight limp, Stormy was in good health and condition. Better yet, Stormy seemed to know he had arrived at a safe harbor.

Stormy had limped into his life last August late one night during a Phoenix "monsoon." The rain had been coming down in solid sheets, the wind blowing it across the yard. Arlen was out on the front patio letting himself get soaked by the summer storm, loving the warm wetness, searching for any sign of electricity in the neighborhood. A yellow-pearl glow from lights in other parts of the valley bounced off the underside of the cloud cover.

In his side vision, a movement startled him, as he had his gaze stuck in the clouds, so to speak. It was just a slow, unsteady shadow making an erratic path. Then, out of the darkness, this mutt appeared on the front lawn and flopped down. It didn't move, just breathed labored breaths and looked up at him.

After the flop-down came the whimper. This was not a little puppy, it was a pretty good-sized dog, somewhere between a spaniel and a shepherd. So it was not a puppy whimper. It wasn't one of those "pet me" whimpers. It wasn't an "I want a biscuit" whimpers. It wasn't even a whimper of "gosh, I knew I shouldn't have pooped on the carpet or eaten your slippers." In short, it was a whimper that justified some decent human empathy. An "I hurt bad" whimper.

So, despite his desire to remain unattached to all sorts of obligations and commitments–and the possibility of being burned, Arlen hunched down close and held out his hand. If the critter tried to bite, he'd have to call Animal Control. If not? Well, the nose did its sniff thing and then the tongue licked the rain off his hand, so how could he not respond? As he began to pet the animal, it winced and involuntarily withdrew. That's when he noticed the deep gash on the shoulder, rain-soaked blood starting to cake in its fur, and abrasions on the legs and torso. The wounds appeared fresh, with blood beginning to coagulate at the surface of each wound. Good thing this wasn't an afghan hound or there'd be a huge, matted heap to handle.

Arlen touched it gently. "There, there, guy, looks like we have to put something on this."

With the dog being shorthaired, Arlen saw that there was no collar. *Hmm. How do you keep a dog still while you go for the salve or peroxide? Well, I'll just have to risk it.*

"Stay here, guy, and I'll be right back."

He went into the bathroom and sought out first aid for humans and pooches, returning with a plastic bowl of warm water, a few washcloths, scissors, antibiotic ointment, peroxide, gauze and his headlamp.

No need to worry that the mutt would go anywhere. There he was, this poor wounded refugee, looking like another step would bring on end-of-life. Iowa farm-boy history reminded him that animals rarely growl when they sense that you are trying to help them. *Androcles and the Lion* revisited.

"So, fella, you know I'm not gonna hurt you. Take it easy, I want to feel you all over first, okay?"

He moved his hand gently across the back. The welts formed a regular accordion pattern, crossing the body from side to side, as though the animal might have been held while a beating occurred. He pressure pointed some spots and didn't find any broken ribs. But, as he fingered each leg, he noticed some smaller cuts and welts there. How could anyone in their right mind do this?

Arlen welled up with anger at some unknown perpetrator out there, probably in his neighborhood, who had taken out his craziness on a small, helpless soul.

He gently washed the gash on the shoulder, smooth-talking his way into the dog's trust. "I'm just gonna wipe the blood off, fella, and we'll see what we have here." He clipped some of the matted fur away so the wounds could be seen. "Did a tree fall on you?" The gash was different than the welts, and seemed more recent. Did the dog freak out in the storm and escape into the night? Did a car hit him during his torturous trip away from terror?

The rain subsided. Arlen thoroughly cleaned the wound and ran his fingers over the unharmed parts of the body: head, face and tail. He was trying to pet the dog without causing pain.

"Well, guy, looks like you'll be staying the night with me. I think we should give you a name, even if it's not what you used to be called. In fact, I hope it isn't. How about Stormy? Suits the circumstance, no?" He stroked the ears gently. The dog turned its head to lick him again and the tail wagged a little.

"Stormy it is, then. Stormy. Welcome to my place, Stormy. Glad to make your acquaintance, though I'd have preferred that it be in kinder times." *And then I wouldn't feel so drawn to you.* Was this critter invading his unfettered loneliness?

"Let's see if we can get you inside. Can you get up?"

Coaxing didn't do it. Arlen placed his broad, wet shirt-sleeves under furry shoulder and rear and hoisted Stormy into his arms. About 50 pounds. Together, they found the soft, dirty red-and-black shag rug near the living room couch that was normally reserved for bare human feet and popcorn bowls. Arlen unfolded Stormy onto the rug. More wagging of the tail. Probably a healthy sign.

Arlen ferreted out a handle-less frying pan from a kitchen cabinet, filled it with water, and placed it by Stormy's head. The dog lifted his head slightly, took a few laps, and lay back down.

The electricity came back on. Conan O'Brien was making wisecracks on late-night TV. The HVAC resumed with a surge and air moved about the room. But Stormy seemed unfazed, cherishing a dry, soft spot without a beating. He wagged some more.

"So you think I should spend the night on the couch, do you? Well, I guess, just in case … Better I'm here to help you go outdoors than both of us being sorry."

Arlen changed into dry clothes, locked the house, and

flopped down on the couch. He woke several times in the night to see if Stormy was okay.

By morning, Stormy had regained some strength. The dog could get up and follow him out to the back yard. The newfound sidekicks both took a whiz on a nearby bush.

The first weekend in March, Rosie, Sam, Tony, Arielle and their friend Chris filled up the guys' two trucks and Rosie's Jeep and hauled their first load to the farm. They had enough chain-link fencing and poles to fence off a sizeable yard for the chickens. Next run they'd bring the chickens in, if construction was complete. They dug postholes for the coop, put in the chain-link fence and set up a set of roosting rails and laying boxes for the hens. Rosie and Sam waved good-bye as the other three headed back to town, confident they'd made a dent in the work and expecting further progress.

It wasn't clear what the sleeping arrangements or relationship would be. Rosie had hardly known Sam when Tony and Arielle had introduced him. Now he was the one staying until Tony and Arielle could come out next weekend to stay. Rosie decided to approach it straight.

"Hey, Sam, with just the two of us here, besides the dogs, looks like I'll get the largest bedroom. You can take your pick of either of the other two or the loft."

Sam looked at her in surprise. It wasn't so much that he found her especially cute (though she was), or that he was interested (which he wasn't — at least not now). It was how quickly she had established her boundaries and a little of a 'landlady' hierarchy by claiming the biggest room.

"What? You don't want me to keep you warm?" he quipped.

"I have Brutus and Bella. And the fire. Thanks for the offer though. I'll keep it in mind." She didn't want to be mean or hostile to Sam. But she did want to sleep alone. Sam was definitely not her type. Rosie sighed inwardly. She wondered if she would had been able to handle it if Chris had decided to stay at the farm. His mess of dirty blond curls and muscular torso stirred her blood. She was secretly glad he wasn't staying at the farm. Didn't know how she felt about him. She wasn't ready to sleep with him, and that's what he'd probably want. Not yet, anyway.

So they put their stuff in separate rooms. Sam decided, since it was still pretty cold at night, to sleep on the couch in front of the fireplace and keep the fire stoked all night.

The second weekend in March, they had planned their first "Build and Barbecue." There would be about ten guys and a few more gals, and by the end of the weekend they could terrace the field, fence it, and bring out the chickens. But on Friday Arielle had to work at the café, so the deal collapsed and only Tony and Chris came. Still, they brought the chickens and got them safely into their coop, with places to roost, laying boxes, a trapdoor for in and out.

Rosie and Chris went to check out the well. From the well, she and Danny and Dad had, years ago, run a PVC line up to the water tank above the house that both flowed into the house and ran separately to the chicken coop. They primed the pump, Rosie tried the rope to start the motor. It sputtered.

"Here, let me give it a try." Chris's extra strength got the motor going, but it still took a long time for the pump to build the pressure needed to pump the water all the way up to the tank. "You might need a new motor," he commented as they trekked up to the tank to check the velocity of the water pouring into it.

"No," Rosie answered, "it's just a slight glitch. It'll run forever. My dad could make it work. I'm getting it checked over and we can just get a new cord or ignition switch or something."

As they walked down the hill together, Chris put his arm around Rosie's shoulder. Maybe they could have a quick night together, as long as she understood he'd be staying in town. He started to move his hand down around her waist.

"Not now, Chris, we have work to do," Rosie said as she flipped his hand away. God, that was startling! It felt really good to have his hand slide down her back to her hip. She felt an urge to just turn to him and ask him to stay in her room tonight. She longed to have his hands move over her body and be pressed close to him.

But she was repulsed at the same time. She would lose control, he'd harm her, he'd do things she was afraid of. And of course he'd consider her a slut, or, if she resisted, a prude. Either way he'd dump her. She couldn't risk that. It wasn't that his work wasn't valuable. It was that the terror of being violated welled up inside, right next to her urge for passion, and made everything ugly.

So, the living room got crowded. Sam invited Chris and Tony to share the floor in front of the fireplace as the warmest place in the house. The three guys made a man-cave out of the living room while Rosie tucked herself under a huge down quilt in the bedroom with the dogs at her side.

Sunday, over breakfast, Tony broke the news. "Rosie, I hate to break it to ya," he said, stuttering in one of those 'I really don't want to say it' hem and haws, "but the reason Arielle didn't come is because we're not going to do the farm here. She needs the money from the café, and we got offered a deal of staying on someone's farm while they're away this year. They already have chickens and are growing hay just outside Prescott. She can keep money coming in and I'll work the farm. We just can't do it here."

Sam jumped on him. "What? You're bailing? Some kind of friend."

"It's okay." Rosie cut him off. This was just like another betrayal. She'd have to be strong, not be taken down by it. She steeled herself. Having the rug pulled out from under her, not being able to count on people, feeling like she was on her own was a familiar pattern. She was tough. She'd had to be. She could handle it. "So you guys won't be part of Clear Creek farm this summer. That it?"

"Yeah." Tony studied his dirty boots. Longer than necessary. "But we'll be out some weekends, you'll see. You know, neighbors helping each other, farmers are a community, and all that. We've already helped you get off to a good start. You'll do great. We'll come out sometimes, and we'll see you guys at Farmers Market."

Chris tried to soften the blow. "I'll come out a little more often, and I can bring some of the other guys. My construction jobs are not exactly regular, and I really like it here. You have a beautiful place." He hesitated, looked away, awkward.

Rosie studied Chris. She'd given him a real brush-off yesterday, though she liked him. She'd like to see him around more. But she was also afraid. She let him create some space for himself. Right now, she wasn't really interested in anyone at this point. The farm was what mattered.

"Well, you're welcome to come anytime. Obviously, we'll need all the help we can get. Right, Sam?"

"Damn straight, Chris. You're a stand-up kind of guy. Anytime." He lifted the coffeepot off the stove and filled the mugs. "Well, we have a few more hours to get things done before you go back. Whaddya say, Tony, now you owe Rosie and me some blood labor? Let's start the greenhouse."

Rosie had to hand it to both Chris and Sam. Both of them kept an upbeat spirit through the morning. The guys started framing the greenhouse while she took the dogs on a scouting trip up the creek for herbs growing naturally on the farm and in the wilderness. She had taken seed samples last year of cliff rose, periwinkle and shepherd's purse. Prickly pear grew in large patches, the flesh good for drawing poultices. Yucca thrived just downstream off the property. Across the meadow grew an abundance of mullein, aka *verbascum thapsus*. Manzanita, piñón and mesquite all offered medicinal properties. Come May, spearmint would flourish in the creek.

On the way back, she walked up the hill behind the house across from the field. Deer and cattle had trodden several trails. Both animals walked close to the horizontal when possible. Her mom and dad had always let the rancher upstream run his cattle through the farm. Folks cooperated like that. The cattle hadn't done any damage so far. Of course the cattle made their mark. They'd have to fence in the vegetables come summer. But if you wanted a walking path, the cows would make it for you. Just cut the brambles and branches away from waist high and above, and your work would be done.

Following the trail slightly uphill, she came upon a clearing among oaks, locust and juniper. Rosie scanned the horizon. The oaks had not budded out, and the view through their bare, crooked branches revealed receding layers of mountains: green, blue and hazy purple touching the early spring sky. It was so peaceful here, so far from any of the troubles that she had tried to leave behind. Squatting on her haunches, Rosie visualized a yoga routine that could include greeting the sun in the east, the south, and the west. The entire hill could include a maze of meditation paths that were discretely marked, for any wanderer to enjoy solitude.

She staked out an area, about 12 X 15 feet that could serve as a flat place for a group sharing a yoga discipline. She might even build a platform, or a shelter with a roof and open sides or large windows, if time and money permitted, for a small cabin. It could serve as a sleeping hut, a project workspace or a yoga studio in the winter.

She fell into quiet. Perhaps from her yoga discipline she could reach into her inner soul and find the calm that so escaped her in the conscious world. African dance allowed an exuberant abandonment of constraint, but she still needed more understanding. Yoga might offer a vehicle for such inner knowledge.

Brutus and Bella exuberantly shattered her calm. They had romped up the hillside, ignoring the path when animal scents took them astray. Finally, they had arrived and set their tongues to work on her face and their tails to wagging in the wind.

"You are my best solace, babies." Rosie chuckled and together they returned to the house.

When Tony and Chris left, Rosie began to feel depressed, but Sam stayed upbeat and determined that they'd make a go of it. "Let's each take a day in town this week," he suggested. "We can turn up some folks to help finish terracing the field. I think Chris has an eye for you, and I can get some guilt time out of Tony. Professor Pete said he wanted to come out, and he'd bring Chloe. Not to worry, young lady, we'll get it done."

After stacking the camping gear, Arlen assembled tools that might be useful for fixing a motor or a pump, or farm crises in general. Ratchet set, pipe wrenches, a few loose fittings, the battery-powered drill (with numerous interchangeable parts), screws, bolts, washers, an extra pull cord. Working at a hardware store had its benefits. To the pump pile he added an 18-inch chain saw, work gloves and a shovel. Just in case.

"Stormy, you and I will have a nice little adventure. She's got two dogs, and if you can all get along, there'll be some squirrels to chase." Arlen threw a large blanket onto the pile. He opened the garage door, packed up the back of the truck, drove it inside, and was ready for tomorrow.

Stormy, *this* man's best friend, lay right now, loosely leashed, in the shade under the orange tree on the front lawn, tail gently wagging, tongue lolling out between the lower front incisors. Arlen wondered: *did he deserve Stormy's loyalty?* He thought about that. Loyalty. Left the family. The bad history he'd rather forget. But they hadn't been so loyal to him, so it turned out better to leave it behind and avoid bitterness over internecine warfare over who got what. He didn't keep up with the old high school crowd. Broke up with girlfriends. Didn't finish college. He couldn't rate himself up there on the loyalty-meter. Why did he feel so comfortable getting it from–and giving it to — this stranger of a canine who had simply dropped in?

82

Chapter 9

The crash had receded from his memory when Casey came into the Club Deportiva this spring. By now, he had a life of his own, a few friends. He and Casey talked a lot about sports. Eventually, Casey mentioned hunting.

"Hey, a couple of us guys've been talking about buying some guns 'n' ammo at the next gun fair at the Coliseum and goin' out to target practice. Interested?"

He hadn't thought much about it.

"What do you have in mind?"

"Well, you know Conner and Sergio, right? They have a friend, Alfonzo, who's gone hunting with an uncle over the years. They were talking about getting some rifles, maybe a pistol or two, and going out to the practice range by Lake Pleasant. Might come in handy someday. Self-defense. Be pretty interesting, whaddya say?"

Well, he couldn't find much against the idea. He really didn't have much going on in his life besides the bar. Had another go-nowhere relationship with some woman. She'd been attractive in a gaunt way. Turned out the reason she liked him was the fast sex and discounts on liquor. The boss had found out he'd been giving her occasional free drinks and nixed that. After several weeks of a lot of sex, he'd gotten tired of the booze. Didn't seem like she could do a blowjob unless she was plowed on scotch. He really didn't like drunken women that much, come to realize. One night when she downed a whole fifth he smacked her up against the headboard. She freaked out, ran to the bathroom, and vomited all over the toilet. He made her get dressed and paid for a taxi home.

He'd gone with Casey and Sergio to some Suns and Diamondback games. For a while, he and Connor had played for the bar on a men's slow-pitch softball league. He liked it. A lot of Hispanics. They brought families. The families would picnic while the dads played. If he wasn't going to have a family, at least he could be around some. Children didn't interest him anymore. Most of the wives didn't either. Besides, there were too many easy women at the Deportiva.

Anyway, Connor and Casey and Sergio all seemed like okay guys. Shooting? Target practice? Not something he knew much about, but he'd learn. Sounded like solid guy stuff. Something to break up the monotony. Why not?

"Sure, why not?" So they set up a time the next Sunday, and went to the gun show.

Thousands of people milled about gawking at thousands of weapons. Definitely not all one type. Every kind of dress, from Western dude and dudette to survivalist to little old teacher ladies, lawyers and construction workers. The Arizona gun laws were lax. Just about any adult could buy whatever he or she wanted.

The others discussed their options in excessive detail. What was the right firepower, whether it was for hunting elk, bringing down doves, or killing humans? Couldn't believe the energy that went into this. He'd long ago lost a lot of his anger. Except against some of the women he fucked. Hadn't gotten him anything but juvenile detention and DUIs.

But they were having a great time. And Alfonzo had hunted big game in the past, or so he said. Sergio was more into what he might use on the street, "if necessary." Casey was feeling up the barrels of some rifles. Conner seemed fixated on the variety of ammo that could be employed.

Ultimately, they all bought something that could take out small game or more at about 300 feet or so, and a few weeks later, they all popped into Casey's heavy-duty Chevy pickup and wound up at the Ben Avery shooting range off the I-17 north of the city, near Lake Pleasant.

Wearing headsets against the volume, he got used to firing a 22 and a 12 gauge shotgun. Not big weapons, but reasonable weight. Turned out he was a pretty good marksman. After the introductory round with the 22, he hit center or second circle on the bull's-eyes and close to the heart on every human-shaped target. The other guys were impressed.

"When fall comes, we'll have to get hunting licenses and get ourselves a few elk," said Conner, who seemed to think the life of a hunter might be much cooler than hanging sheetrock.

He remembered the farm. God, it was beautiful. If only he were still part of the family. Well, it was probably abandoned. The parents were dead and *she* had gone to California. Her brother Danny lived in Flagstaff. Even when they were alive, they didn't go there that often. Now probably no one went there. He could probably make sense of the Forest Service roads. Not that complicated. Not many turnouts. He'd be able to take them to this place with a cabin, a stream, and a forest. Even though the family had kept their acreage as a 'wilderness preserve,' he and the guys could start their hunting exploits right on the property if no one was there. The guys would really be impressed.

"Say, I know of a place in the Bradshaw Mountains outside of Prescott. Lots of deer. Some people I knew had a farmhouse there. It's been deserted for a few years. Isn't the hunting season about October?"

Casey caught the reference. "I remember. Say, you're right. No one probably goes there anymore. The girl – she went to California, right? Let's plan a hunting trip."

Sergio joined in. "Let's make a plan for fall, then. A few more weekends here at the range, maybe some summer hikes, and we'll be all set. Cool."

So he went up in their estimation. He added something

to the bargain. There it was. Plans to have a few hikes in the summer and some hunting in the fall. His life wasn't so empty after all.

Turned out, Arlen was the next one to visit Clear Creek farm after Tony and Arielle's dropout. Rosie had texted him about her needing go into town to bring in some feed for the chickens. Having a pickup and friends in Prescott Valley, he agreed to come up Friday night, stay with them, and meet Rosie in the morning to collect supplies and feed.

Rosie stayed overnight in town with Arielle and Tony. Rosie brought her guitar, and the girls strummed and harmonized into the night. Tony went out with the guys for beers while the girls stayed home.

"How's it going, Rosie?" Ari asked. "I really didn't expect to have this other opportunity come up. I'd really looked forward to living with you this summer. But Tony thinks the farm we'll move to will be a better deal. And I can keep my town job and some money coming in."

Rosie was not going to act disappointed. "It's good. We've gotten a lot done. Chickens are in the coop, field getting terraced. Sam and Chris and Tony got a lot done."

"What's with Chris? I was sure he'd hook up with you. Why'd you turn him down? He's a looker, Rosie. You could do a lot worse than him. I mean, you could have him as your weekend man-slave if nothing else. Don't you think he's hot?"

So the gossip mill already had her giving him the cold shoulder. Damn. Couldn't anyone keep their business to themselves?

"I figured he'd be here in town and probably have a lot of other girlfriends. Don't you think he's already seeing someone? Wasn't he seeing someone this past fall?" Rosie tried to put the blame, if there was to be any, back on Chris instead of feeling like she should sleep with anyone that everyone else thought she should.

"He broke up with her," Ari answered. "Gee, it was just that I thought he liked you and you liked him. Doesn't have to be every night, you know. You could still have something going."

"I have a hard time with sharing," Rosie replied. "If he's in town, I'm sure he'll find another girlfriend in a heartbeat. You wait and see."

"Well, what about Sam? I know you don't know him well, but…"

"Ari, are you trying to find me a fuck-buddy? I mean, I do not have to sleep with any guy just because he's at the farm. Why don't we change the subject?" Rosie was getting the eerie feeling that everyone thought she was weird for not sleeping with the nearest unattached guy.

Maybe she *was* weird. You could call it moral standards, but the fact was that while she found some guys – like Chris – attractive, the whole sex thing disturbed her and left her with vague, unnerving dreams. Some nights they were right-out nightmares.

"OK. I was just trying to be friendly," Ari murmured. "Say, Rosie, what about a few harmonies before hitting the sack. OK?"

"Let's sing some Dolly Parton, Indigo Girls and the Roche Sisters. We've already memorized some of their best."

Ari strummed chords, Rosie plucked. Ari sang a soprano melody and Rosie harmonized. They let the subject go and finally came back together as friends. When Tony came in later they were both asleep, Rosie on the couch, with her arm over the neck of the guitar.

Next morning, she met Arlen at his friends' place. Rosie didn't have Bruce and Bella with her, but Arlen had Stormy. And Stormy wanted to know who the new person was. He sniffed. She held out her hand. Then they made friends.

"Good-looking dog you have there," Rosie said, as Stormy accepted her hand on his fur.

"And he has good taste in ladies," Arlen responded, letting Stormy hop up into his passenger seat. "Don't know quite what I'd do if I had to carry a human passenger in the truck."

"Someone would have to have him on her lap, wouldn't she?" teased Rosie. This dog seemed pretty alert.

"What's the story on him?"

"He landed in my front yard one rainy evening," Arlen said, as he closed the door. "We've been fast friends ever since. Rescue dog. Had welts and cuts all over."

"So you patched him up?"

"I couldn't leave him out in the rain. God, Rosie, you couldn't believe how bad the bruising and bleeding was. I'm glad I was outside that night, or he might have died."

That explained the bond. She knew about abuse. The fact that Arlen had taken in a stray and nursed him back to health added to the positive vibes. But for now, they had shopping to do.

"Let's get to the feed store, then the hardware store, and we'll be ready to head on in. Do you want to follow?"

Even though he knew Prescott and Prescott Valley, he let her lead. She seemed more comfortable showing him what she knew, and he was glad she was acquainted with the area. He wasn't really interested in babysitting someone who had to ask for help on everything.

Together, they did a quick run for supplies and threw some heavy sacks into the back of his truck.

"Wait, Rosie. Before we go to the farm, I need some breakfast."

"That's fine, I need another cup of coffee. What do you have in mind?"

"There's a Town Market with chorizo burritos," Arlen said.

Rosie chortled. "The Town Market? Cholesterol City! Why don't we try the Whole Grain Café? The fare is much better there."

"Speak for yourself." Arlen knew she was right, but he had long satisfied his unacknowledged loneliness with comfort food. It showed around the middle. He realized that she knew it, but he wasn't going to let her turn into his personal food cop. "Besides, Town Market has great coffee. Shade grown from a Costa Rican co-op."

"But, it's so …" Rosie started to say, but she stopped. He was right. The coffee was great there. And besides, who was she to tell this near stranger what he should and should not eat? So they grabbed a bite to go and tag teamed down the long dirt road, pulling up to the farm shortly after 10 a.m.

Sam walked over from the chicken coop thanked them for the supplies. "Ah, my chicks will be so happy," he laughed, hauling the sacks out of the truck to refill the chickens' feeders. He was glad Rosie had some help, but he wasn't sure about another man on the place. Could break up the partnership. Better keep a watchful eye.

Meanwhile, Stormy met up with Brutus and Bella. After some initial growling and species-appropriate discovery motions, they banded together to harass the chickens. The humans had to fend them off. After a few parries, the canines discovered that the creek and the woods were free from human interference.

The guys spent the morning terracing the field, hauling boulders from the creek to make the embankment between levels more secure and navigable. Rosie made a pile of sandwiches. Seemed like the guys got along. Maybe a sign of things to come. At noon she rang the old brass bell on the porch and they broke for lunch.

"I haven't forgotten about the well, Rosie," Arlen said as they polished off the chocolate chip cookies for dessert. "Remember? That's how we met, and I want a shot at that motor."

"Well, of course, Mr. Expert. Show me your stuff."

Sam busied himself again in the field, and Arlen hiked with Rosie to the well. He took some of his tools from the truck bed. "Brought some odds 'n' ends. Just in case."

She pulled the cord on the motor. No luck.

He pulled the cord, and there was a sputter. "I think it's low on gas, or the fuel mix isn't right," Arlen said, starting to tinker with the ignition and then the carburetor. "The power seems really weak."

"I disagree. I think it's fine. It'll be fine," Rosie argued.

Arlen fiddled with the switches, pulled the cord a few more times, and they got it going, but it took a long time for the pressure to build up. "Are you sure you don't want me to take it into town and have it looked over? It may be due for some major repairs. You might even need a new motor."

"No, no, I'm sure that's not it." She sounded so determined that Arlen backed off.

As they waited for the tank to fill, they propped themselves against some boulders by the creek. The muddy brown spring run-off cascaded high against the banks and swirled by, energetic and laden with upstream detritus. Minutes passed, just sitting quietly, watching the flow, sensing its natural power.

"So, did you tell me you came from farming?" Rosie finally asked, as if there had been ice needing to be broken. In truth, she had felt only warm comfort sitting next to this guy she hardly knew. But that in itself was the problem. Maybe talk would create a safe distance, in the guise of friendliness.

"Yeah, I grew up on a farm. Went to the school in town and sort of grew to expect more from life than the backbreaking routine. Hog business changed from raising them for market to prize showing, and with my brother wanting to take it over, I needed to move on. Got a little more education. But," he paused, lingering over some of the childhood memories, "I liked the animals. I learned about all the equipment. The open space, the routine, they stick with you. Like here," he waved his hand out toward the meadow. "I like this. I could camp, work, do the farm stuff for a bit. But I don't think you'll catch me trying to make a living on a farm again."

"Well, so far *I* like it." Perfect way to maintain a slight distance from this guy with rough, warm hands. He did not try to put one of them on her. That made his company easier. On the other hand, was there something wrong with her?

Arlen had picked up on the slight distancing. Hmm. Interesting. Was it her? Or him? No rush, though he was curious about the static over the pump. She wasn't looking at it realistically. Something other than the pump, totally unrelated to him, was going on. Again, there was time. Stormy and the 'Bs' were hitting it off. He didn't have any other big interests. Not quite looking for a big relationship. The dog was enough. Though he did like the way she tackled the field, the coop, the equipment. And the way she loved her dogs.

The comfortable quiet returned for a while. Then Rosie said, "Let me show you around a bit more. We can check the tank to see if it's full. If so, we can come back and shut off the pump, and then I want to show you my latest idea up the hill."

There. It happened again. It was easy talking with him, so she was ready to roll out the fantasy brewing quietly in her head. Oh, well, it wasn't like he had any control over her, or the place. It wasn't dangerous to talk a little.

When they inspected the water tank, disappointment set in. It was only two-thirds full, even though they had allowed plenty of time.

"I dunno, Rosie."

"Well, we'll just give it a little more time, that's all. It'll be ok."

She took hand clippers from her back pocket and they meandered up along a switchback. They arrived at the clearing a little out of breath. But what really took Arlen's breath away was the view. Almost three hundred and sixty degrees. Today was virtually cloudless, with just a few spindles of cirrus. If there was a God, God was here in these forested hills.

"Wouldn't this be a great site for a yoga platform? I've been thinking that we could, without too much effort, clear the brambles and make some other trails up and around this hill. There are enough fallen trees that there are natural logs to sit on for meditation, and folks could wander in solitude without fear of getting lost."

When they reexamined the tank, it had filled. They shut off the pump.

"Come, I have one more place I want to show you." Rosie led him across the field, up the other side of the creek, and into the pines.

"This is where we scattered Mom's and Dad's ashes," she said softly. "They loved it here. I sit with them almost every day, and I feel some solace that the wind is keeping them company." She sat on the slope of the hill.

Arlen rested on his haunches a few feet away.

"You didn't tell me about your folks," he said quietly. "I'm sorry. What happened?"

She looked out across the field.

"They were killed instantly in a car crash almost two years ago on the I-17. So it's just Danny and me. They left us this place. It was more of a retreat for them, but I think we can make it a farm."

Arlen started to realize that he was watching a future unfold that grew from a painful past. "Have you ever worked, like, for a full year or so on a farm?"

Why would anyone choose farming? It was so grueling, so difficult to make a living. The weather was constant in its fickleness. With Rosie, he surmised, it was the past she wanted to escape. A farm seemed to be one way to do it.

"No ... Ah, no. I spent some time on a few farms. But I've been around folks who have run a farm. And Sam has. I studied botany and sustainable farming in college. And I know this place. I know we can make a go of it."

There it was again, that edge of determination laced with something sadder, some untold story. He let it drop.

That evening, they lit a fire in the fireplace and Rosie took out her guitar. Arlen knew some of the songs and sang along. He tapped a hand drum left in the living room. Sam made percussion from bones, rusty horseshoes and nails. They all collapsed, with the dogs keeping them company, right in front of the fire. Arlen stayed awake the longest, watching the embers slowly fade.

Chapter 10

The next weekend, as promised, Danny came in with Hotchkiss and they plunged into gold dredging in earnest. Rosie had to laugh. Granted, he had his restaurant in Flagstaff, and it looked liked they were going to expand it into a larger venture. But when Danny came to the farm, he was all about finding gold. He had acquired all the fixtures that made the machinery work. And he now had wore his rubberized boots and long-armed rubber gloves so he could work the dredge and not get soaked or frozen in the process.

"Say, Sis," Danny ventured, when they cut the motor. "None of my business, but any romance on the horizon? What's the scoop with Sam? You guys are here alone most of the time."

"Danny, she's too classy for him," Hotchkiss interjected.

That was a surprise. Hotchkiss had mainly stayed in the background. Rosie felt a prickle of protectiveness from her brother's pal.

"You're right, Hotchkiss. I'm too classy." She tossed a clump of mud at him. "But you're right about another thing. We're not an item."

"How does he feel about that?" Danny asked. "I think he'd have to find you – ah – attractive. I'm sure he admires you."

"I made it quite clear right off the bat." There it was again. So quick on the draw, putting men off. No subtlety or assuaging of male egos. Rosie bit her tongue in regret.

Hotchkiss smoothed it over. "Danny, didn't you say Rosie's here to make the farm work? I say let her have her priorities. I mean, it's not like you or I have a wild and fantastic love life either. Especially you." He picked up Rosie's idea and tossed some mud Danny's way.

Danny decided to get back to the dredge. Hotchkiss and Rosie seemed determined to gang up on him. "Should we break it down and take it back to the house today?"

"I want to work it tomorrow and find gold myself," was Rosie's vote.

"Nah, I think we can work it tomorrow too," Hotchkiss added. "Anyway, I'm off right now to start up the wood-burning stove and make some dinner. Ok?"

"Good idea. Let me know if I can help." Rosie picked up some of the loose tools. "I appreciate your taking over some of the dinner chores. Sometimes I wind up being cast in the domestic role."

Hotchkiss picked up the rest of the tools. "If there's any female I know, Rosie, you are the one person who should not be typecast. Everything I know about you from here and from Danny says you're one of a kind. That's a compliment."

Rosie blushed. Danny wondered if Hotchkiss had his eye on her. But no, Hotchkiss had a sometime girlfriend back in Flag. And if there was one thing you could say about Hotchkiss, it was that he was a loyal friend. Wouldn't mess with anyone. Especially his best friend's sister.

The evening's menu was barbecued chicken, refried beans, sliced tomatoes and a can of corn. Not too fancy, but good after a day at the creek. After cleaning up, the three of them, she and Danny on guitars, Hotchkiss on the drum, Rosie adding vocals, made a rockin' trio. Sam made it a quartet by adding percussion.

Over breakfast on Sunday, Danny put it to her. "Sis, do

you think you're really going to make it? I mean, it seems that just between you and Sam, you're understaffed, so to speak. I can't help much, but I just want to check in. You feeling safe up here?"

Sam chipped in his two bits. "Danny, we've got more help than we realized. And we've gotten a lot done. Rosie's can swing a pick and pack mulch like nobody's business."

Rosie fed off Sam's vote of confidence. "No worries, big brother. Sam here is a real farmer, and he also knows his weapons. Plus, the dogs are the best early warning system you could ask for. And count on." She stroked both at once. "And, besides, we've lots of help. On some weekends we've got guys from Prescott coming in — Tony and Arielle have helped, they have a pal named Chris, and Professor Pete and his girlfriend Chloe have come out once and helped too. And, by the way, this guy I met at the hardware store, Arlen somebody, he and his dog came out. He's pretty nice, and handy. Got the pump working a little better. He thinks it should be replaced but I don't."

"He might be on to something," Danny mused. "I've really struggled getting that thing going the last few times I've tried it.

"No," Rosie disagreed. "I think it's okay. Dad could handle it. Just needs a little tending, that's all."

Danny let it drop, since his pump for the sluice box worked fine. He didn't get much of a read on Sam, except that he seemed to be a pretty hard worker and did what was needed. Everything was on course. Warm weather was heading their way. But he still worried about Rosie and Sam being here alone most of the time.

Picking up on it, Sam invited them down the field to have a morning target practice. "Let's take everything we've got," he urged. "Let's see what damage we can do with this stuff. Yee-hah!"

Their arsenal was impressive. Sam had acquired an AK-47 at a recent gun show, and from the family they owned a .30-30 and a 22. Rosie had somehow picked up a .38, and Danny had bought a Glock in a pawnshop. They set up some bull's-eyes on the far hillside for practice.

Using mufflers, they each took a turn on each of the weapons. Rosie opted out of the AK-47 semiautomatic and Glock after one try. Too heavy. Sam showed off and put some tin cans out in the field, picking them off and making even more of a racket. Danny proved a fine marksman on every weapon, but he took to the shotgun.

"Next time I come out, I'll bring a skeet shooting machine, so we can practice for dove and turkey hunting. Just joking, I know we don't hunt at the farm. But skeet would be fun. A moving target."

Hotchkiss agreed.

"Great," Sam chimed in. "More the merrier. We've found that if we make a little noise on the property, people know we're here, and we're armed. Not so likely to mess with us, right, Rosie?"

Sam had a point. Since they'd either started target practice, or fired their rifles in response to other gunshots in the forest, fewer strangers trespassed.

"So Danny, think little sister is safe enough with all this protection?" Rosie asked.

"Well, lil' sis, as long as you keep your head on straight, it's cool. I'm impressed with your aim. I guess you'll keep each other's backs."

Hotchkiss concurred. "Danny, you must've raised her right. She really knows her stuff. I think they're handling it pretty well."

They wrapped up the target practice and headed over to the creek for another hour of dredging for gold. They put some of the gravel in a bucket to search later for flecks of the precious, elusive metal. Finally, they hauled the dredging equipment back to the house and made themselves sandwiches on rye, with lettuce, tomato, mayo, mustard, gherkins on the side and a huge bag of sour cream potato chips.

"Anything you need before I take off, Sis? I can come back next weekend if you need me."

"Nope, it's pretty good for right now. Another crew's coming up for Memorial Day weekend, about five or ten folks, and that should really help us stay on track. I'll cell or text you if I really need help."

After a restless night at home, Wainwright threw the covers off his mattress and rose gingerly. Joints creaked. Muscles slowly recalled their purpose and stretched toward readiness for another day. The TV was on, some daily show with a pretty young announcers in proper dress and tidy hair, yakking about the weather and recipes.

It wasn't quite summer here in Flag. The drum circle hadn't started up yet. He missed it. Missed the rhythms, missed the men. Wondered about that young woman. What was so familiar? Why had he noticed her? Why had she looked back at him? His mind was so weakened, so distracted, his memory shot. Why couldn't he put a finger on it?

He limped over to his reloading factory and laid out some powder and casings to make some new rounds for his .45. He took a handful of old brass casings, and de-capped them. The .45 rotating turret for .45s was in the clamp. He would set the used casings one by one in the die, swing the arm of the turret machine, and pop out the pin.

Next, he took a handful of de-capped casings and dropped them into the vibrating case cleaner. The cleaner was a small tub filled about seventy per cent full of a media of crushed corncob, walnut shells and ceramic bits. He turned on the cleaning machine and the casings were gently sucked down into the sandy media, jostled and vibrated.

The cleansing process usually took about two to three hours. He stared at the current batch for a few moments, mesmerized by the smooth swirling of the disappearing brass. Then he turned his attention to a batch he had recently sifted out of the media. This batch was already cleaned. In contrast to the powder-stained ones just dropped into the gray, sandy mixture, these casings were bright and shiny brass again.

He set the clean ones in the shaker. His shaker was a blue sieve with slits large enough for any sand mix stuck in the casing to exit, but small enough for the casing to remain. Sort of like a lettuce shaker used to remove excess water from rinsing. As his hand turned the blue shaker, the excess media, which had been stuck in the bottoms of the casings or their primer niches, shook out of the sieve and fell into the gray pot underneath.

He moved back to the rotating turrets in the clamp with the arm lever. He set a casing in die #1, swung the arm, and the slightly bent casing was realigned into a perfect circle. He swiveled the set to die #2 and set the casing in place. For his .45s he used a Federal primer of silver. He removed some from their box on the shelf and dropped several into a little plastic dish. The dish was set on the turret and had a feed into die #2. With a swing of the arm, the primer was pressed, gently but firmly, into the small hole on the bottom of the casing from which the previous spent primer had been removed, and from which all media had been shaken loose.

He was ready to add powder. He used *Modern Reloading, 2nd Edition,* by Richard Lee, to ascertain the exact amount of powder required for the casing of a .45. This was his bible for ammo making. You absolutely had to be precise about the amount of powder, and what type, you added to a particular caliber casing for a particular bullet. You never mixed powders–that could be a disaster when you fired.

He found the number needed and attached the powder holder to die #3, secured the casing, swung the arm again, and the exact amount of the correct powder frop-fropped down through the hole into the casing.

He then placed the copper rounded shoulder bullet on top of the casing, pressed down on the arm, and the round pressed firmly into place atop the casing. His bullet was done.

Wainwright looked with pleasure on the shiny copper-brass combination. Finally, he set it in the digital caliper. It had to measure no less than 1.264 inches, or 32.12 millimeters in length. The caliper flashed at 1.264 inches. It was good to go.

Wainwright repeated this process for two hours while the other set of casings were shedding their powder and taking on a new sheen. He made a good supply for himself, several dozen. He packed seven in a clip and the rest tightly in a small cardboard box that had been used for the original set. His military sidearm, his old, old friend, was ready to fire.

But you couldn't fire it here in town.

Wished he had a place to go, or a ride to get there. There was plenty of forest, but his hip had never recovered from the shrapnel wound. A good long hike over the hill past the Lowell Observatory northwest of town, something that was easily manageable for a while after 'Nam was now, in his sixties, painfully hard work.

He threw an English muffin in the toaster and heated water for instant coffee. Had a Camel while waiting. Took a long drag. Couldn't smoke while he made ammo, so this puff was welcome. Another good, old friend.

Wainwright poured sugar and powdered creamer into the hot brown liquid. Tasted rotten but kept him going in the morning. At least the butter and jam improved the muffin. Though it had to compete with a cigarette. Ultimately, he didn't taste much.

After reloading and breakfast, Wainwright felt the need for something. A walk, another cigarette, seeing someone, buying a burrito, a small bottle of vodka or a cheap six-pack. Something his meager vet's disability dollars could afford.

Hotchkiss was restocking the little shelves in the Kachina Convenience Mart when Wainwright entered, looking like he hadn't changed clothes in a few days.

"Hi, Dubya, where ya been?" He smiled and stuck out his right hand — the one without breath freshener packs in it — toward the vet.

"So it's still Dubya, is it?" Wainwright asked. "Ya know, I hated that president. Dumb shit. Didn't know anything about the Middle East. Pain in the ass."

"Couldn't agree more, but I kind of like how it rolls off the tongue for you. 'Dubya, Dubya.' More friendly than 'Mr. Wainwright, sir.'" Hotchkiss made a fake salute to emphasize his point. "So … Okay?"

"Okay, man. If you say so." Wainwright bowed a little,

conceding that if Hotchkiss liked it, it felt okay with him. Hotchkiss had been a real pal, truck pooling him to those drum get-togethers on the way out to Mormon Lake, out where nobody cared if there was a flask or a joint in the mix. No Flagstaff cops swooping down on anything left of uptight, clean 'n' white, super right.

"So what brings you in today?" Hotchkiss moved back behind the counter to help another customer buying some Gatorade and popcorn. "Haven't seen you in a bit. Winter okay for you?"

Wainwright shook one leg, then the other. "Stiff. Cold 'n' wet doesn't make you feel that limber. Need some serious hot toddies to keep a body warm." He kept his hands in his oversized military coat pockets, which he wore despite the warm sun over this Memorial Day weekend. "Still cold, even when I come inside. But the main thing is, there isn't much to do."

"Tell you what, Dubya. I've got a friend, and we go out to his place in the National Forest sometimes to dredge for gold. It's quiet out there. A creek, room for target practice. We even shoot skeet sometimes. Maybe we can go out with him and pan for gold and shoot some skeet one weekend. Name's Danny. Wait, I think you met him. We may have drummed at his house last fall. Got a sister and some friends up there trying to make a sustainable farm with organic chickens or veggies or some damn thing. I'll ask him. You'll remember him. He's got drums and a guitar."

"Yeah, think I do." Wainwright shuffled awkwardly. Wasn't sure how other folks would take to him. But Danny, he remembered now. Good guitar work, friendly sort of guy. "Sounds nice. Sounds real nice."

"Danny should be coming by any day now, so I'll ask him. He's got a 4X4 and so do I, so we're covered for the drive. Got any camping gear?"

"Got a bedroll and a sleeping pad. Target practice, you said? Maybe I'll bring my 12 gauge and my .45. Practice on some skeet or whatnot. Wonder if there are wild dove or turkeys out there. Could use a shotgun on them."

"Well, now, take it easy, Dubya," Hotchkiss cautioned. "Don't want to overpower them all at once. I know you were probably a sharpshooter in the war, but this is mostly a bunch of kids and a farm. They have a shotgun you could borrow. How about you stick with the pistol?"

"All right, all right. But while I'm here," Wainwright recalled, "ya got a six-pack on sale, or a little flask of Smirnoff? And maybe a burrito? I'm hungry. Man's gotta eat."

Hotchkiss threw a banana, an apple, some beef jerky and a small bottle of cheap vodka into a sack of extras that he added to Wainwright's purchase of a burrito and beer. Didn't mention the extras or charge for them. Hell, this guy served and was wounded. His life looked pretty shot since returning from Vietnam. Hotchkiss rang up the burrito and a six-pack of Coors Lite, the cheapest he had, took the ten-spot, and handed Wainwright the change. "I think this'll tide you over for a bit. Come on back in a few days. I'll catch my friend Danny and see if we can go out to his farm some weekend."

"Thanks, Hotchkiss. You're a pal. See ya soon." Wainwright headed out the door.

April up at Clear Creek farm sped past with several rainstorms. Some starters in the greenhouse were growing well, and by early May the Farmers Market had opened. Rosie and Sam sold all the eggs and their tomato starter plants. At the end of Saturday Market they'd high-five. They were starting to make a return on their investment.

Arlen had come up once early in May. The dogs had enjoyed each other, but he and Rosie sparred over both food and the motor. He brought food she labeled as junk and he complained that the pump really needed an overhaul, at least. Their last parting was cool. They promised to keep in touch, but a few weeks passed without a cell message. He had texted that the "heirloom, cage-free organic eggs" tasted delicious, but it was a generic friendly message with no plans for another visit. Rosie focused on work and preparing for market.

On Memorial Day weekend, Tony and Arielle promised to come out Saturday after market, and Chris said he'd come too. The new guy, Jack, was around as well. He claimed to have construction skills. Maybe he could help start the platform up on the hill that she fantasized could be a yoga retreat space.

Benny Whitehorse, a Navajo, had become part of the group that hung out in town after Farmers Market. Benny was from up on the rez around Tuba City, but here in Prescott he was taking EMT classes at Yavapai Community College. Said he wanted to return to the rez and make a contribution of modern medical skills for his people. Too many folks relying strictly on the traditional medicine men, and some serious malnutrition and lack of modern care going on. While he expressed a deep connection to traditional ways and values, there had to be a place for better medical care in his people's rural nation carved out of the northeastern corner of Arizona. He was quiet–very different from Professor Pete, who knew a lot and shared it. And different from Jack, who talked too much, didn't know much, but who acted like God's gift. Chris was the only one who kept her interest as a possible guy to date, if he was still around when she could declare the farming venture a success. But she'd have to get through harvest season first.

B enny rested his strong brown forearms on the monster maul. How had he gotten himself to these mountains? It was not part of his plan. But they were all swapping tales at Farmers Market last Saturday as some gals sat behind tables full of spring herbs, and Chris from his class in human anatomy had talked up this place in the mountains outside of town and how they could build a barn or a chicken coop or a goat shed or some sustainable thing.

Chris introduced him to Sam and Rosie, who were selling tomato starter packs and organic eggs. He noticed Rosie right away — a seriousness at the corners of her eyes that seemed older, somehow, than some of the folks around her. Like some of the wise women on the rez. Women who'd been through things, who knew stuff. Didn't necessarily want to talk about it, but were wise about the ways of life.

Sam started talking about the farm. It sounded like way too much work for two people. That's why they were hoping for a few folks to come out and help. Several of the guys were going out for the weekend, work, eat, generally have a good time, and–who knows? Benny had not met a lot of Anglos who were so inclusive. It felt ok. And he liked the idea of getting to the mountains. So he went.

Benny liked Prescott. He liked being in a city where there was reliable running water and electricity, where there was a good grocery store, and where most of the people weren't dirt poor and too dependent on an unresponsive bureaucracy. His people constantly struggled, in a poor land, against the BIA. He contemplated the many disparities between life on the rez and life here in a *bilagaana* – white people's – town. More than that, he contemplated the cultural differences between the prevailing white culture and his conflicted Navajo ways.

So many rich cultural and spiritual traditions, yet so much poverty. From his mother's clan were several talented weavers, from his father's were silversmiths. But when you counted up the benefits, it seemed that poverty was more of a grinding set of hardships than a beautiful "way of life" that was so often extolled by Anglos and the current tribal leadership. It was confusing, enriching, and painful all at once. No wonder too many of the guys his age self-medicated with drugs and alcohol. It blurred the feeling that they were mere grains of sand in a desert of forces more powerful than any of them could handle.

So Benny moved to Prescott and studied Medical Technology. He hoped it could help his people, but it had already helped him. He liked the technology of it, even the blood. And he liked helping people. He felt especially drawn to emergencies and the trauma unit at the hospital, where all the med tech students had a rotation. He liked that it was different. Even though he missed home.

The caravan of two trucks had entered the forest service road early Sunday morning. Chris and Jack rode in the cab of Chris's truck. Tony and Arielle sat with some building supplies in the back. The professor and a woman named Chloe drove the other truck. Benny rode by himself in the bed of their truck, sitting on one side with several sheets of plywood and some 2 X 4s on the other.

The first four miles were paved, then four of gravel. Then the next three or four were forest service dirt roads, sometimes smooth, sometimes like a washboard or full of potholes. Forty-five minutes later they pulled up at a low-lying log house with a veranda surrounding it on three sides. The porch looked out on a large sloping meadow scattered with mullein stalks that stopped on higher slopes overgrown with scrub oak, walnut, juniper and ponderosa. The well-named Clear Creek gurgled nearby.

"Hi, Chris, glad you're here," said a short, curly-haired girl holding two big dogs by their collars while everyone hopped out.

"Hi, Rosie. Hi, Brutus. Hi, Bella." Chris swung out of the driver's seat, slamming his door and patting the dogs. "Rosie, you remember Benny, and Jack? They thought it would be fun to come help out with the barn raising, or barnstorming, or whatever you've got going this weekend. We brought food." He pointed to the truck bed and Tony helped Jack lift the cooler out onto the ground.

"Keep the top closed," warned Rosie, "or the hounds will finish dinner before we even see it." She gave Chris a quick sweaty hug and extended a hand toward Benny and Jack.

Instead of shaking hands, Jack looked her up and down. She was slender, with a nice figure, clear complexion and stunningly blue eyes. The tank top let show firm tan muscles, cleavage and firm little breasts, and no extra fat. A few dark curls had escaped the bandana and left an intricate shadow along a graceful cheekbone. She wore low-slung cut-offs that revealed a flat abdomen and muscular thighs. She must be advertising, Jack thought.

Benny frowned. Clearly, Rosie had been busting her chops

in the field and didn't need to be viewed as a piece of meat. Isolated or not, this place was a place where people had put their time in making the road passable, fencing off a chicken coop, terracing the field. Not a place where you treat a hostess with disrespect, even if you are coming to provide some free labor.

The cultural difference between the *Dine* —his people — and the *bilagaana*, showed in greetings. Where he'd always look down a bit and wait to be greeted, the Whites were much more informal with stares and hugs. It appeared that there was a freer sexuality here, not that the rez didn't have its fair share. But it also looked like there could be abuse, misreading of signals, an invasiveness that set him on edge. He'd keep an eye out on Jack.

Jack gave a big smile, pushing back his ball cap. "Pretty place you have here, sweetheart."

It was 80 degrees in the sun but a chill hung in the air. "We work here, if you didn't notice." Rosie released Brutus. The canine made direct inquiries of Jack's rear end. Bella sniffed Benny.

"Nice to see you again you, thanks for the invite." Benny accepted Rosie's hand, hoping to change the tone. "Handsome pair of dogs you have there. What are they?"

She relaxed and gave Benny a dirty but civil handshake. "Brutus is a Lab/hound mix, and Bella is pure Pitt Bull. Brutus looks the part and barks. Bella can be very friendly. But don't cross her."

Sam came over from the field and started another round of hellos. "Hey, Tony, Arielle. Hi, Chris, Jack, Professor, Chloe, Benny. See, Rosie, I told you they'd come." He gave big grubby hugs to his friends and a solid handshake to Benny.

"Hey, Benny, glad you could make it."

Sam looked the personification of a hayseed. He sported a set of striped overalls over his bare chest, with dirt-crusted feet at the bottom. Straw-colored strands of hair protruded from the edges of an uneven leather hat, banded with sweat.

"Pretty serious spread here." Benny noticed that Sam had affected a Southern accent.

"How're the EMT tech classes going? Maybe you can be our medic for the weekend. But no one ever gets hurt." He smiled happily.

Benny looked at Sam's bare feet and wondered how long that would last.

"How about we spend some time chopping wood?" Rosie wanted to get the ball rolling. "Idle hands are the devil's playground. We can stack some by the back of the veranda and then put another stack next to the fire pit in the meadow. In good weather, we cook and eat there." Without wasting a step, Rosie handed a bear-toothed saw to Jack and pointed to some pruned apple branches piled up by the drive. "Benny, how would you like to try your hand at splitting the wood from that ponderosa over across the creek?"

"I'll give it a shot," said Benny. "Got any work gloves?" Instantly, he felt dumb. Of course she'd have some, and of course he should have brought his own.

"Help yourself. There's a basketful on the porch."

At least she didn't seem to need to put up her guard around him. Too many years of watching his sister endure abuse from drunken male relatives, he didn't want to be seen as the enemy. The way he felt, he wasn't.

"Suit yourself, softie," Jack scoffed. "I don't need any. I've got a *man's* hands." Benny caught the hint of a smile on Rosie's face as she explored the innards of the cooler for dinner options.

Arielle and Tony headed for the chickens and Sam took Chris to the field to set up the irrigation pipes that would feed the crops they might plant this weekend.

Professor Pete took Chloe around for a tour along the farm's fenced boundaries. His daypack sported a clipboard and bags for seed and plant samples. They would probably be the least useful weekend 'helpers' in a practical way. But they might have long-range ideas. Benny was interested in seeing how the whole operation was going, but he'd do what was asked of him just now.

The great thing about a monster maul is the wide axe head.

Benny landed the blade in the middle of the old, fat ponderosa stump. The tree had died either in a fire years ago, or more recently from the bark beetle infestation. Huge 150-foot trees just dried up and died. A harsh winter and windy spring had brought them colliding into stronger trees, sometimes catching, sometimes breaking, ultimately crashing to the forest floor. Others had been removed against the hazard of fire. A chain saw had buzzed the trunks into two-foot movable sections. Dozens of logs lay around in the field, awaiting his maul and a move to the fire pit.

The logs had 12- to 18-inch diameters. Benny took a full swing, thighs and waist and shoulders bringing the maul back, then landing it square on the upturned section. The blade would enter and smash it into four or five parts. Just like that. The desiccation from fire and blight eased the job. In an hour he had cut a full cord of light but handy firewood, great stuff for the fire pit. Tonight there would be burgers and a bonfire. He rested on the maul and let the breeze blow off his sweat.

Across the meadow the apple trees cast dappled shadows across the creek up the bank. Jack, stripped to the waist, was cursing at the apple branches, dry but hard, that resisted his large-toothed saw and sometimes snagged against knots. Jack hadn't even figured out how to make the cut with the branch over a stump, letting the end fall away from the blade. Benny imagined blisters welting up on Jack's *man* hands.

Benny liked Chris–a pretty reliable worker with multiple construction skills, but who had dropped out of the college to work and take care of his disabled father. He had taken an anatomy class at Yavapai, probably to understand his dad's predicament. Arielle was terrific on the guitar and harmonized a lot with Rosie, but she didn't bring much muscle to the project. She did seem good in the kitchen. Tony had a lot of muscle and the machismo to go with it, but was too quick on the verbal draw on any topic, from building a storage shed to what the weather might do.

Tony and Arielle had loaded some supplies, plus Jack, into

the bed of Chris' pickup. Jack was, like Chris, also a dropout. He lacked both academic smarts and solid construction savvy but was a regular at any barbecue or beer fest. There might be free food, beer and women, so he said yes to the work weekend.

Professor Pete looked very much the part, with a salt-and-pepper beard matched by salt-and-pepper ponytail behind a balding forehead (covered by a "Think Green" ball cap), a Grateful Dead T-shirt and cutoffs. "Pete," as he preferred over "Mr." or "Professor," offered expertise in seed collections and forest regeneration, too esoteric for the weekend's outlined projects of fencing the field, framing a work shed, chopping wood. But perhaps he was worthy of an educational fireside chat Saturday night.

Chloe worked for the Yavapai County Extension Service. She had a medium build, bronzed body. She had increased her endurance by doing clearance work undertaken by the Forest Service on dead trees throughout Northern Arizona. Chloe sported an 18-inch chain saw in the back of Pete's truck–a guy-sized machine. Maybe she'd use it to section a few fallen trees.

She was a bit of an Amazon-tigress mix. On the one hand, she could do as much as any man. On the other, she wore a bikini top and short hiking shorts that revealed tight breasts and long slender legs. As she headed downstream, she looked ready for a romp in the woods.

Chloe and Pete headed away from the group, on a 'seed-search' mission. They came upon a rocky waterfall that fell into a deep long pool pouring out over a small sandy beach. "Hey, Pete, let's strip and have a skinny-dip in this pool." She didn't wait for an answer.

"What if anyone sees us? I have a reputation to defend."

"They are all working hard at helping Rosie and Sam. And besides," she coaxed, "this may add to your reputation. C'mon, try it." She laid her clothes in a neat pile and slid horizontally into the dark water, avoiding any rocks that might jut up from the bottom.

Pete did likewise and soon they were naked, wet, and

thoroughly enjoying themselves. "Say, Chloe, would you be interested? I have a little blanket in my pack."

"Honey, just say the word. I thought you'd never ask. But let's find a place a little more secluded and smooth." They donned sneakers and took their clothes to a mossy glen surrounded by oak and bushes, surprisingly hidden yet with room enough for two.

Pete tugged her blond braid and pulled her down lightly. She climbed on top of him and they made love slowly, riding up and down, feeling the patterns of sunshine through the leaves on their naked bodies. Chloe shook her breasts in the air and came with a delicious shiver. Pete followed immediately with several vigorous thrusts.

"God, you could just get horny all the time, being so free here," she said, after they lay quiet for a moment.

"My beautiful extension worker, you are truly a wild woman. I love you," Pete declared, as if to the universe. They could have shouted and no one would have heard them.

"Say, Pete, it's none of my business, but do you think Rosie and Sam have found paradise here?" Chloe began to dress, picking grass and leaves out of her underwear.

"I'd hope for the best for both of them, but, you know, I don't get the feeling that that's what they're about. Sam seems pretty engaged in the farm project. Rosie, well, I don't know how to put it, but somehow she seems…"

"A little stand-offish? I noticed that. I thought it was just me. I guess if the one guy you sweat with in the dirty fields twenty-four-seven is not the one you want, you have to establish your boundaries."

"Maybe, but I can't help thinking it's something else. Anyway, none of our business. And, anyway, if she takes to someone like Chris or Jack, we'll surely find out."

"I don't think it will be Jack. Did you see the freeze she put on when he eyed her up and down?"

"He was a little unsubtle. Uncouth, even, I'd say." Pete dressed and put the blanket back in his pack.

If anyone noticed the grass and straw in their hair when they returned for lunch, no one made any mention of it.

Despite the midday replenishment of huge ham sandwiches, chips, a mound of grapes and some brownies, the sun wore on everyone.

Around two o'clock, Jack nudged Tony.

"How about we take a little drive back upstream for a break?"

Tony corned Pete. Pete waved Chloe over. Arielle sidled up. Chris dropped his pickax and joined them.

Pete invited Benny. "We're going to take a short break. I hear the creek has pockets of gold. We're going upstream to investigate possible mining claims or places to put a dredge. Who's in?"

Jack, Tony and Arielle chorused "Sure," and Chris and Sam agreed. Benny nodded silently.

"But," queried Chris, "shouldn't we ask Rosie?"

"We can tell her, but let's not give her too much notice. I really want a break, not a lecture on the farmer's work ethic," Jack wisecracked, not wanting to lose momentum for the venture.

Chloe added, "If we go in the truck, we can get back faster and help with dinner or the chickens."

"Besides," mused Arielle, "Rosie has just gone inside to take a break herself." Menstrual cramps and a migraine didn't need to be mentioned in mixed company.

They piled into Chris's truck, Chris and Arielle in the cab, the rest in the bed. Brutus and Bella, deep into a canine siesta, didn't flinch or even raise an ear.

"It's just about a five-minute drive, but you can walk back along the creek bed in fifteen. Could be a nice stroll around dusk," reasoned Chris as they backed out of the drive to head up the hill.

"Rosie, we're just going upstream for a bit," called Arielle. No one knew if she heard.

The truck rambled slowly along the dirt road. The road went up a hill and down, and then took a short curve back toward the meandering creek. Freshets from the springtime runoff spurtled into the creek. A large broken branch stirred a vortex of cloudy swills around a deserted dredge-hole.

They hopped out. Professor Pete brought out a plastic bag and scooped seeds off some dry wildflowers. He pocketed some samples and penciled identifications on his clipboard. Jack displayed a little plastic bag as well. "Anyone interested?" He proffered some "Colombian gold" and rolled a joint. There was general approbation as some took papers to roll one or two more to share, and Chris flicked a Bic to light up.

Back in the house, Rosie heated water on the propane stove for some chamomile. The kitchen was soothingly dark and much cooler than the porch, which sported a temp of 82 degrees Fahrenheit in the shade. Must be almost ninety in the sun. She poured a steaming mug and then diluted it with ice from the cooler. Hosting a work crew was handy, if for no other reason than they supplied fresh ice. Otherwise, the only things that got chilled in the summer were beer and soda cans set in the creek.

She let the dogs out onto the porch, closed the bedroom door, let the curtains flutter through the open windows, nudged off the work boots and sweat-soaked socks, and fell back on the bed. She leaned over to the bedside table for an elasticized sleep mask, left over from a long-ago overnight air trip to France.

The mug cooled a bit. Propping up on an elbow, she added a little tincture of periwinkle to the tea. It was supposed to be the answer for migraines. Wouldn't it be nice if it knocked her out for an hour?

For Rosie, teas and tinctures were ok. Drugs – prescription or otherwise – were not. Fear of addiction and her experiences of inability to control events around her, were deterrents. Consciousness, memory, awareness, control were essential. She couldn't handle any more invasions, any more surprises, any more losses. Drugs would turn her into a big loser. A loser, a failure, a victim that she was determined not to be. But Rosie still longed for sleep. Her migraine throbbed, her abdomen cramped. She wanted a few blissful moments of forgetfulness. She sipped the tea, donned the eye pads, and lay down on the bed, pulling a light coverlet across her torso. She closed her covered eyes and sank toward sleep.

Instead, a set of disconcerting images swam into her mind, appearing as if in a "yes, no, maybe" Magic Eight-Ball, vaguely at first, clear for a moment, then fading before you could read a clear answer.

The target practice with Casey, Sergio and the guys had whetted his appetite. This was guy stuff. He wanted more. He found a shooting alley in Phoenix, rented ear-pads, and practiced with the .22. Found himself visiting the shooting gallery every week.

Thinking about the place in the woods triggered a memory. Hadn't there been talk of gold mining in the creek? Didn't the father have some kind of dredging equipment? He surfed the Internet and found information on placer mining — mining in water — and then looked up gold mining in the Bradshaw Mountains. He even visited the public library and studied some history, mining methods and mining maps.

Maybe they could take some pans with them and pan for gold. A little informal effort. If it worked, they could return for more. So what if the land didn't belong to him? There was no one there to know the difference. Maybe he'd find a few real nuggets and cash them in. That would take the worry out of working at the bar. He'd have a cushion in the bank. Wouldn't feel this nagging anxiety about life that seemed to haunt his off-work hours. He was sure they'd find at least one of the things they were hunting for. Guns and gold – this would be a good trip.

Chapter 11

Tony had brought a six-pack. They walked down to the creek to rest. A few moments of silence set in as folks chugged and inhaled.

Benny had declined. "Maybe later."

Just better not to start. Can lead to too much trouble. He'd had to bail out too many relatives from the Coconino County jail to feel good about any of it.

"This whole mountain range has a long history of mining for metals," Pete mused aloud. "There are maps that mark every claim, both along the creek and in the mountains. Take a look at the sign posted on that cottonwood. Thunder Mountain Mining Claim. No Trespassing.' They've been mining this section of the creek for years."

Chloe kicked a few rocks into the creek in disgust. "They have no respect for nature," she complained. "Think they can go anywhere and just dig up the creek and then leave it desecrated. It's criminal."

"How's that?' asked Tony. "They look like they've been around for a while. If it's criminal, why doesn't someone do something? Why wouldn't the Forest Service get the Feds on their case?"

"It's not illegal," Pete replied. "In the West, we're stuck

with what's called the Mining Law of 1872. Yes, 1872. Here it is now the twenty-first century and we're still operating under the same outdated law from the 1800s. But you could call it criminal. Chloe's right. They can stake a claim, dredge their section of the creek, and do a lot of damage to the landscape just to get a little gold or silver. Then they leave the hillside scarred or divert the original flow of the creek. Mining can really disrupt the normal patterns of local plants and wildlife. I don't think it's right."

Benny held his tongue. He knew about the 1872 Mining Law, at least as it had applied to some major incursions by mining companies who had Federal contracts to do massive explorations for heavy metals under the surface of tribal land. The minerals included radioactive ore that had polluted local water drainage outside Tuba City and over near Four Corners. It was dangerous business, but the Prescott folks weren't in the same league as the tribe, so he kept quiet.

The joint circled a second time.

Arielle collected the empty beer cans and put them back into the carrier. "Well, I don't understand why they have to leave these huge ten-foot potholes along this stretch of creek. It's not the natural lay of the land, is it? And they can just leave it like this?"

Pete offered his expertise. "The law says anyone who finds anything 'worthy of a prudent miner' can have a claim on a part of a creek, and they supposedly don't have to 'restore' it until after they're done. They could take decades. Since the government supports mining generally and with Forest Service people in short supply, there's no enforcement. These guys can pretty well do what they want."

Arielle spotted a cylinder of corrugated metal about three feet in diameter and eight feet long. "What's that?"

Sam explained. "It's a culvert. Part of the supposed obligation of folks with a mining claim is to keep the road passable in the vicinity of their claim. This claim runs about 1,500 feet along the stream. See where the road crosses the creek and there's a sharp drop-off from spring flooding?"

He pointed upstream about fifty feet to a gouge in the road.

Someone had dumped some gravel and broken branches in the stream to improve the crossing. "Right now you could barely make it across without four-wheel drive. If we have another serious run-off from winter snows, or heavy monsoon rains this summer, the road could be shut off even in four-wheel drive low. I bet the culvert is part of a plan to fix that part of the road."

Jack challenged them. "Well, how long has that rusted piece of junk lain around here? It's just another example of disregard for nature. We're all about keeping the environment clean, right? Why should they be allowed to clutter up the forest just to suit their gold-digger's greed?"

"And look at the bunch of broken beer bottles scattered around that fire pit," Chloe added. "Bunch of slobs. We could teach them something about respect for the forest."

"Ya know," Jack added with a chuckle, compliments of his latest toke, "the farm could use that culvert as a water tower. Get it back to the field uphill from the well, place it behind the trees so it doesn't show, solder a bottom, top and spout on it, pump water up the hill, and it could serve the farming operation when they have to irrigate the veggies."

"But it's not your water tank, it's their culvert," Benny said quietly.

This wasn't right. Ball Cap and Ponytail were just off track. And Extension Girl should know better. Dope and booze were making these guys self-righteous and wrong.

"No one has been here in months," Sam argued. "I drive the road pretty often to get supplies in town. I haven't seen them at all. I'm not even sure that thing is theirs. I don't know how it got here."

"Yeah," Tony chimed in. "How does anyone really know when to fix the road? Sam and Rosie could really use it now for a water tank. Couldn't you, Sam? And we're all here and can help them." He looked around the group for support.

Arielle nodded naively. Chris gave a "Yeah." Chloe added, "They're the bad guys anyway." Even Professor Pete, smiling rather contentedly, assented. "Not a bad way to recycle useful materials. You can use everything on the farm."

"So how're we gonna get it in the truck and back up the hill?" asked Jack. "Everyone onboard?"

"I'm walking back down the creek," Benny said.

He started off on his own. He felt a huge distance between himself and these *bilagaana*, these white folks who touted themselves as loving the forest but who didn't respect other people's stuff. Weird, unsettling. He set out alone.

"See you back at the farm," called Arielle. "You'll like it once it's there, you'll see."

For a minute everyone gazed after Benny, a little surprised. Then they all smiled.

"Wow, what a plan!" Chris laughed. "Groovy, such a find. Wow!" He enjoyed a round of grins.

"Let's haul ass," Sam ordered. "We gotta make time before sunset."

They scrambled to their feet, backed the truck up to the culvert, and hoisted the tin chimney into the bed of the truck. It bounced like a washboard and finally settled quietly until they started driving and it rattled some more.

Sam said, "Chris, you and Jack and I will sit in the bed to hold it in place. Who's willing to walk back? The road takes five minutes, the creek takes less than ten."

Tony and Arielle agreed to hoof it while Chloe jumped into the cab with the professor. Pete put the truck in drive and they headed back.

At first the figures in the dream lacked form and color. They were only vague impressions of blackness shading into grays. Rosie might have been in full sleep. But shapes emerged, pressing themselves slowly onto the scene, colors seeping in, first dusky, then brighter. Animals emerged at the edge of a hunter green stand of trees–wolves, wolverines, mountain lions. All predators. From the high branches flew hawks, vultures, all in browns, purples, against a burnt orange sky. Slowly, deliberately, the specter of death strode forward, a bony, hooded figure in a death-colored cape that covered the face, or the skull, that dragged bony feet and cape on the

116

ground. In its stark white hand swung a huge steel-gray machete, a sharpened blade glistening with putrid florescence, swinging methodically, with menace.

She finally saw a female figure, an emaciated child, clothed in a swirl of Provencal blues, yellows and greens. The girl was standing at a bridge, back to the railing, with a thunderously violent river roiling below. A fall over the rail would mean certain, bloody, mangled death. Staying on the bridge would result in the terrors wrought by the specter, vultures and wolves. She felt herself inside this girl-figure, in it and of it, not the same, but merged, at one with her.

As space evaporated between the girl and the robed skull, the girl's hollow black mouth uttered an Edvard Munch scream, open, soundless, suspended in space and time, eyes holding terror, hands up to her ears, blocking the sound of the specter's slashing blade and the pack's ferocious howls. They were coming closer, closer, the distance shrinking. She was screaming louder, louder. But there was no sound. No one could hear her cries for help. She leaned back against the railing, caught between two terrifying deaths.

The creek spread out on the flat downstream. Despite a few good spring rains, it shallowed out, and Benny used boulders for a footpath. He accelerated once out of their sight, sensing a chill settling in the late afternoon.

He heard the scratching before he saw the front door and came upon Brutus and Bella trying to get in. He sped up.

"What's up, guys?" he queried, as he opened the front door.

Inside, Rosie sat huddled on the couch, wrapped in a large cotton cloth of sienna, teal, and ochre. It looked African. She was shivering and staring out the window as if she had seen a ghost. Yet it wasn't cold and no one was there. It was still well into the high 70s.

He almost said something, but that pained and hollow look on her face resonated badly in his memory. It was the look his younger sister had after an older cousin had gotten her alone at a large tribal pow-wow. The look of one from whom something so precious was taken and for which there are no words of consolation. His sister, sure. It was so hard to prevent, when there was so much alcohol on the rez. But Rosie? He didn't know her, and it didn't seem like it could be true. But the deep, blank stare was unmistakable.

Brutus and Bella knocked Rosie back on the couch, slathering her face and pawing her body for attention. She snapped into focus and quickly hugged them both. At first, she wasn't aware of him. He remained still and silent. Rosie looked at him, at first not seeing, then with a flash of anxiety. Benny did not move. He knew of a desecration, and he kept silence to honor that knowledge. He quickly looked down, the Navajo way, as if he hadn't seen. But he wanted to let her know he was holding her safely in the space where pain abides. He bent down to pet Bella, who came running back to make sure his presence was acceptable.

The voices of Tony and Arielle broke the silence as they sloshed down the creek. Then Pete's truck rattled and bounced across the rocks and water up the field to the tree line.

"What's going on?" Rosie asked, back in the now.

Benny hesitated. "I'm not sure," he equivocated, balancing between the peace of Rosie's momentary ignorance and his own uncomfortable awareness of the truck's cargo. "Do you want me to…?"

But the truck had rolled up the hill above the field, dropped its cargo, and rambled back to the house, everyone laughing at their clever gambit.

"Boy, do we have a great surprise for you, missy," Jack began, eyes still dilated.

"We've righted a wrong, zapped the greedy miners," Chris added.

"And," Pete broke in, "cleaned up the environment."

"Wait, wait, wait," Rosie challenged. "I am sorely confused here. Just what did you do?"

Benny didn't want any part of this. "I'll start the fire for dinner at the fire pit," he interrupted quietly and left to get supper started. No one heard him.

"Let's show you," said Tony. "You will sooo get a kick out

of this. Jack and Chris thought of it. It's such a great idea."

"What's such a great idea?" Rosie's cheeks were flushed with anger and uncertainty. What had they done, without asking her?

Chloe took the lead. " It's cool. Let's walk up up to the tree line."

Together, the entire entourage trouped uphill. Hidden among a huge juniper and several ponderosa was the corrugated cylinder, rusted to a "fit-right-in" brown and standing on end. Walking by, one might have thought it was the fat trunk of an aged oak tree.

"That's a culvert!" Rosie exclaimed. "Where did you find that? We didn't have one of those. Where on earth …?"

"Not a culvert, Rosie, a water tank," Chris explained, as if it were elementary. "We can solder a bottom onto the cylinder, add a spout, and presto! We'll have a water tank for the drip line to the vegetables." He stood next to it, hand on the side, as if showing off a felled grizzly.

The Professor tried to sum it up. "You have to admit it's a great recycling of available resources."

"But where did you get it?" Rosie persisted. "We didn't have one, and you didn't bring one in from town. Where did you find it?" She was beginning to realize it had come from somewhere in the forest.

Arielle piped up. "Rosie, it was a cool find. Remember where there's a mining claim for Thunder Mountain upstream? Well, while you were taking a nap, we went out to explore, and there it was, pretty close to the road. Looked so old it couldn't belong to anyone, so we decided to clean up that site and put it to good use."

"But wait a minute," countered Rosie. "If it was at the Thunder Mountain site, didn't anyone think it might belong to them? It takes a big effort to haul stuff out here into the woods. It wouldn't just drop there from the sky. You all know that, don't you?"

Chris quibbled. "Look at it this way, Rosie. Here you are, here we all are, caring hugely about the environment. You've started this terrific farm to show that we can have sustainable agriculture. You've got starters in the greenhouse, spring crops already planted in the field, and eighty organically fed laying hens to produce wonderful eggs for Farmers Market. That other site is just a bunch of miners who are out to rape the wilderness, dig huge potholes in the creek, leave it disturbed, all just to get some gold."

"And besides," Tony chimed in, "we've shown that by using virtually every piece of lumber that was already here at the farm, plus the stones for foundations and borders, that we can clean up the forest, recycle, and put natural resources to good use."

Rosie's irritation simmered. "Didn't any of you think that it belonged to the guys who own that mining claim? Isn't this stealing?"

Jack added his two bits. "They're just miners, Rosie. They're destroying the creek."

"So what? Danny and Hotchkiss are miners too!"

"But they aren't doing anywhere near as much damage as Thunder Mountain." Sam was now on the defensive.

"But the guys at Thunder Mountain weren't breaking the law," Rosie pointed out. "The Mining Act of 1872 says that if you stake a claim, and you work your claim with the 'efforts worthy of a prudent miner,' you dredge in the creek. There's no size limit. I don't really like it, but they weren't breaking the law."

Benny broke their train of thought by sending a huge gong out from the dinner bell. He hollered, "I'm about to put on the burgers. Come and get it."

Chris mumbled. "Wasn't really a big deal. I mean, after all …"

"We'll take this up later," Rosie snapped.

Silently, they trudged to the fire pit. The tokers' bubbles had been burst. It felt really different than anyone had expected, and the THC was wearing off. A little gloom surrounded them.

Folks washed up in the creek. Benny had spread all the fixings on the table, keeping the meat away from Brutus and Bella. Condiments, a huge salad and a stack of buns awaited them. The scent of charcoaled burger and kosher dills drew them away from their debate toward dinner.

After everyone had a plate and sat on a stump or rock, Jack started it up again. "It was harmless fun and, besides, the miners were breaking the rules of the environment. Doesn't everyone agree?" There were several nods of tentative approval. It still seemed like a pretty good idea.

"But the culvert wasn't yours to take. You were all stealing." Rosie repeated very slowly, as if speaking to English-language learners. They needed to understand every word. "You. Were. All. Stealing."

Benny had let the fire burn down to cinders for cooking the burgers. Now he rekindled it. After a few slow catches, it burst into flame. Everyone's face was illuminated in hot orange.

"Well," Chloe continued, looking at Pete for support, "they'll never know who took it. They'll never find it here in the trees."

"Chloe, I'm ashamed of you," Rosie fired back. "Stealing is stealing. They weren't breaking any law, and you all were. And, "her blue eyes glared piercingly through every person except Benny, "this is *my* place. My *family's* place. We have a responsibility to our neighbors. Doesn't matter if you don't totally like what they do. We all connect with each other, and it matters to *me* what our place stands for."

Pete was the first to back down. "I see your point, Rosie," he admitted. "I guess you're right. But it's so big. It'll be hard to return. They won't miss it."

"You got it here, you can get it back. Or you can pay them for it."

Chris softened up. "Maybe you have a point, Rosie. We were a little stoned." He smiled guiltily and looked at the others. "Want to go talk to them about it?"

"Hell, no, Chris, I don't want to talk about it. I," Rosie glared at him, "*I* didn't do it. And the thing is, I *have* talked to them. They seem like okay guys, but there are three of them. They all pack weapons and dress like survivalists. I'm five foot three. I will not go talk to a bunch of armed militarists all by myself, not even with a gun in hand. This is your mess, and you guys need to clean it up."

"Well, they shouldn't be packing so much heat either," Jack parried.

"There you go again, with your damn hippyspeak," Rosie answered. "You can't treat people, who aren't breaking the law, like criminals. We're in Arizona. Anyone can buy just about any firearm they want. In fact, Sam and Danny and I all have rifles, and we have two pistols besides. The fact that someone owns a gun doesn't make him a bad guy. It just makes me really cautious around them. Here we are in the woods, five miles from the nearest house, ten miles from town, and you never know how people will act if they know there's no one around to stop them."

Arielle came over and put an arm around Rosie. "I guess we didn't think too much about it." She sighed. "We can take it back in the morning."

"I just hope they don't show up tonight and decide to take out the thieves who stole their stuff," Rosie zinged. "It's Memorial Day weekend, and there's still tomorrow."

Sensing a lull, Benny stirred the glowing embers to let the fire die down. Ponytail was disappointing, for a professor. At least he was the first one to finally catch on. Ball Cap continued to be a jerk. Rosie really held her ground. Strength in a small package. After what he had seen that afternoon, he felt a surge of admiration for this *bilagaana* girl.

Everyone seemed worn out by the confrontation. The air crackled with discord. Almost no wine or beer went down, and each solo or couple found their place in a tent, in the house or on the porch. Soon they were asleep.

Chapter 12

The softening Monday sky, empty now of fading stars, gave a sparkle to dots of dew lingering on oak and alder buds. As the sun began to bring color back to the forest, the dark of night rolled back down the eastern face of the western hill across the creek from the farmhouse, revealing yellow-green grasses in the field. Behind the farmhouse to the east, the western slope of the hill remained deep in shadow except for a glimmer of quartz rocks outlining the trail that headed upward toward the clearing.

Rosie had slept in her jeans. She peeped out a window, eyed the rock line of the ascending path, donned a fleece hoodie, and quietly slipped out the back door. She held the door in both hands to close it quietly, so as not to disturb the others. She managed to leave Brutus and Bella curled up against a few bodies in front of the hearth in the living room, so they wouldn't break the early dawn calm. Standing on one striped wool sock at a time, she slipped her feet into her work boots, caked with mud, that had spent the night outdoors.

The fire pit argument had been chaotic, disruptive, unsettling. Who were her friends? People she thought had solid values appeared, like leaves in the wind, to be up for whatever current blew strongest. She had respected Chris from his solid

123

work ethic. She had thought Professor Pete and Chloe were old enough to know better. And Arielle, dear Arielle, like a petal in the breeze. At least she realized her mistake and was genuinely sorry.

Maybe it was just the beer and dope. Dope had that name for a reason — it made you stupid. It could be fun. You could think you were cool and had great insights. But in reality, in *this* world, it screwed up your judgment. At least most of them seemed to realize that and were starting to come around by the end.

She wasn't sure about Benny and Jack. It appeared that Jack had sullenly hunkered down, unwilling to admit he was wrong, especially in front of a mere woman. Benny was more of an enigma. He had come upon her after the nightmare. Hadn't said anything, just petted Bella. But he seemed to know something. Was it that he knew about the culvert and was embarrassed? Or was it something else? She hadn't said anything either. The nightmare had sucked her into the center of a maelstrom from which she had not yet awakened. She didn't quite understand him.

The footpath led off to the north, on a gentle diagonal. She remembered the morning Arlen had brought the rocks from the creek bed — only the ones sporting a good chunk of quartz — so they would sparkle against the dark earth. The morning he helped her set the trail, he had seemed to know instinctively how to grade it around some precipitous outcroppings and steep falloffs. He had worked his McCloud, a dagger/bar/spade, between embedded rocks. He had lopped away natural obstacles, like a thick stand of locust bush or a rocky precipice. They had made a trail all the way up the near side of the hill, but still on a gentle incline, sometimes intersecting and making use of the work done by deer or cattle.

Rosie had worked on it the weekend Danny and Hotchkiss spent dredging for gold. Now, after a few zigs and zags, she reached the top of the hill, which she had privately dubbed "the clearing." A pile of kiln-dried #2 pine, hunched under a tarp, lay protected from the weather but ready for construction of the yet-to-be yoga platform.

The sun had not risen behind the farthest mountains in the east. The sky was turning a soft powder blue, with some coral. The saffron sun would rise in a few minutes. Now was a good time to sit in harmony with the hills: the birds that were beginning their songs, the dew was sparkling on pine needles. She faced southeast, to pick up the sun as it began to rise between two peaks on the Mogollon Rim, almost one hundred miles to the east.

Since the night was clear, Benny had thrown his bag down on a flat spot south of the house, facing east. This was so that, according to his people, when he rose in the morning, he could face the sun and praise the Great Spirit for giving him another day.

He didn't see another creature — man or dog — stir. But when he awoke he saw a road to the southeast that curved around uphill. He rose quietly and followed it. The road had been abandoned and now sported several saplings. Deep gullies from heavy rains cut into the roadside edges. Rains did not come often enough, even here in the mountains, but when they came they displayed a power that one should not take lightly. Sometimes, he observed, the *bilagaana*, the Anglos, seemed oblivious to nature's absolute power. They had controlled so much that in their arrogance they lost the ability to prepare for or appreciate the violent storm or flood, or even the extended and pervasive drought, in the course of time. And, in their busy-ness, they often missed the beauty. The trail curved around to the northwest. The light, which had been mostly gray as he ascended, was coming more into its own with hues of blue and pink. Soon the sun would appear, a large golden orb, as if being born from the V between the mountains in the distant horizon.

A flicker of movement caught Jack's eye as he rolled over in his bag on the veranda. There was room for all of them, but a few had slept inside on the living room floor, including Rosie and the dogs.

He was pissed. Who did she think she was, shouting them all down last night? It had been a good idea, and who cared about the survivalist desecrators anyway? They'd had a good time. He had a strong argument. Here was this little curly headed female, not even a year older than him, acting all high and mighty and self-righteous. Arguing until the fire gave up and died.

And the worst of it was, almost everyone caved in, right there, right in front of him, to her face. Well, Sam didn't say much and Tony was kind of quiet, but Pete, the heavyweight college professor who had been so comfortable with their idea — Pete almost led the way. Then, one by one, Chris, then Arielle, and even Chloe. No backbone. Like lemmings to the sea. Well, he wasn't going to admit he was wrong. In fact, he even felt like giving her some kind of payback.

A figure had come out the back door. It had been a soundless exit, but through the glass windows he could see Rosie's blue jacket heading up that meditation path behind her house.

She was alone. The dogs were still inside. She appeared to have left her rifle in the house. Hmm. He remembered the cold shoulder she had given him yesterday morning when he had tried to be nice, tipped his hat and everything.

Had to admit she had a cute little body. Pretty much every curve showed through the tank top and the hip huggers. But she sure didn't take to him. And why not? He was a looker, six feet and no fat, muscles from working out. He had taken off his shirt on purpose yesterday morning when he was sawing those apple branches. She should have noticed. He wasn't short of women when he was in town. Damn! The job had been harder than he expected. Got some blisters. Should've worn gloves, but wasn't about to admit it to anyone, especially her. And he'd come out to this place half-expecting he could get a piece of ass. She wasn't hooked up with anyone. So, why not her?

She was going up the hill alone. This might be an opportunity waiting to happen. Jack slipped out of his bag, carried his Nikes to the other side of the porch, sat on the bottom step to put them on and tie up the laces fast. He glanced quickly back at the bodies on the porch. Not a ripple of movement. He turned and followed her up the hill.

He took the path at first, but then thought she might see him, so he cut into the woods at the northern switchback and headed through an easy spot on the mountain. She had headed back to the southeast, still heading uphill. Careful not to crunch a fallen branch or freshly dead leaves, he pursued her, keeping her petite silhouette either within sight or ear-shot. She was a tease. Look at that ass as she moved. Must be asking for it. He'd make her want some. She'd find out how hot he was, why the women in town wanted him. He'd make her open it up to him.

Thus they continued, hunter and unsuspecting prey, up the hillside, out of sight and earshot from the sleeping bags on the veranda downhill.

Rosie had become familiar with the clearing. She knew its bumps and smooth spots. She had come here before. It was a special place, not one she had shared with anyone else. She savored it as a child who finds a hideaway in a tree or outcrop. She sat easily, sister to the earth.

Yoga and African dance – the two meant so much to her. With the dance, she could escape her emotional cage and move her body into liberation. With the quiet physical and spiritual discipline of yoga, she began to examine that cage more carefully, how it sometimes seemed to wrap around her entire being, yet was somehow invisible.

The nightmare had returned. It was familiar, that little girl trapped between attack and an escape of death. It had shown itself in different colors, different shapes, but was always es-sentially the same. A nightmare in which she was trapped. She felt exhausted by this unpredictable, reoccurring fear that welled up in her consciousness by surprise or invaded her dreams. She wanted to be free of it, but wasn't sure how to move on. Perhaps meditation would bring insight.

First she stood facing east. Slowly she did a forward bend. Then she let herself down gently on the ground. Sitting cross-legged, she cupped her hands loosely in her lap, closed her eyes, and felt the slight warmth of the dawn on her skin. It was almost possible, sinking into this *om*, to forget the past, the desecrations wrought by *him*, the abrupt and terrible death of her parents, the huge anger and sadness and ineffable loss that sometimes swept over her in waves. Here, for a few moments, there was just the scent of juniper and the warmth of the rising sun.

As Jack arrived from the northwest, Rosie was sitting still, facing southeast. He slipped silently into the clearing, and in three crouching steps he sprang upon her. Grabbing her around the body with one hand, he pressed his mouth hard on hers, forcing his tongue into her mouth. He slipped his free hand and grabbed her breast under the fleece, tweaking a nipple.

"You weren't so friendly yesterday," he cooed, "but today you're going to beg for it. You'll love this fuck, little sweetheart." He moved his free hand down between her legs, stroking her clitoris. That'd turn her on.

She was trying to wrestle free. Stronger than he thought. He continued to explore her mouth. She made no sound. "No, little sweetheart. You may be quick with words, but you're going to be moaning right now. C'mon, baby, feel it. Beg for it. I know you want it. You're going to be glad I did you."

Jack rolled with her to the ground, his body on top of her. He unzipped his jeans. He pulled down her pants. She was hot and wet. He was about to slide it into her. Until, as if from nowhere, another body crashed into him.

Coming up from the road at that instant, Benny saw the attack and lunged for the two of them, shoving Rosie aside into the dirt. He quickly had Jack prone on the ground, one arm wrenched back behind him.

"Not on my watch, Ball Cap," he said softly.

Rosie rolled out of the way, stunned. "Benny?" Then she recognized Jack and saw Benny's tight hold on him. Pulling up her pants and hugging the fleece close around her, she huddled into herself for a few seconds. Benny and Jack were both breathing hard. Jack looked the other way, grunting. Benny moved to a sitting position on Jack's back, a knee on his right arm and the half nelson on his left.

"Rosie, will you go down and start some coffee?" Benny conveyed in the fewest words possible that, for the time being, this incident was over and he was in control. He did not lessen his hold on Jack. "We'll be down in a little bit. Wake up Tony and Chris and Professor Pete. Someone will need to leave soon to drive him back to town."

At first, Rosie just sat there, absorbing the scene and studying Benny. It was the first time she noticed his long black ponytail and the scar across his cheek. Then, she realized what Benny had done — why he had shoved her aside and put a lock-hold on Jack.

Benny was focused on his captive, feeling the tension of the taut body under him, waiting for it to surrender. He had no intention of letting up until Jack accepted defeat. If only he had been able to act this fast for his sister. Maybe today made up for something.

"Okay." She rose unsteadily, shook her legs to regain circulation, gave a half wave to Benny, and trotted down the hill. She took the old road, which was in bad shape but more open to view. Almost as if she feared another attack if she came by the narrow footpath she had carved out of the hillside.

Rosie woke Sam first. He was her partner on the farm. He was most familiar, the one she'd talk to if something came up. Sam rolled over, grumbling.

She persisted. "Jack — he tried to... Benny's got him pinned down," she mumbled.

Chris heard the commotion. Then Rosie woke Chloe and Pete and went inside to rouse Arielle and Tony.

"Time to get up. Benny'll be here soon."

By then the dogs were wide awake and clamoring to get out, so Arielle went to the kitchen. Soon, Chloe came in, helping slice up some melon and crack eggs in a mixing bowl.

"Omelettes?" Chloe asked, as Rosie lit the gas under the

coffeepot. Then she noticed that Rosie had grass in her uncombed hair and dirt all down her jeans and jacket. "Oh, my God, Rosie, what happened?"

Silence met her, but a silence that women understood. Chloe put her arm around this petite, wounded person, turned her slowly toward her bosom, and enfolded her in an embrace against harm.

"Jack?"

A nod into her shoulder was sufficient.

They stood quietly at the propane stove until Rosie relaxed. "What about Benny?" Chloe asked.

"Benny's got him. They'll be down soon. Someone needs to take him to town."

"Pete and I will go," Chloe said, and she went outside. Quiet voices told Rosie that everyone now knew. Chloe came back in. "Arielle, can you take over breakfast? Pete and I can do with a cup of coffee. We'll be moving out fast."

"Whatever you leave behind Chris and I can bring later," Tony said. He left the packing to Chloe, corralled Sam and Pete and Chris, and together the four young men strode out to meet Benny and Jack.

Before she started packing, Chloe took Rosie's hands in her own. "Rosie, Pete and I talked last night. We are really sorry about the culvert. We were incredibly stupid. It was the wrong thing to do."

Rosie nodded silently. "Thanks, I appreciate it."

In a few minutes, Benny came down the hill, following Jack and tracking his every move. Chloe had packed their bedrolls. "Benny, could you come with us?" It wasn't a question. "I think Jack will need company in the back of the truck."

"No problem." Benny pointed the direction to Jack and they both climbed into the bed of the truck. They leaned against opposite sides, each propped on a bedroll.

"Coffee, Benny?" Chloe handed a mug to Pete after he was seated and had started the motor. She held out another.

"No, I'm good. The road's a bit rough. But could you throw in two water bottles?" As she did so, Sam and Chris took Brutus and Bella by their collars, opened the front door, and put them inside to keep them from chasing Pete's truck down the road. Rosie and Arielle watched from a window. From the time everyone knew, to the return of Jack and Benny to the house, until they headed out, took less than ten minutes.

Rosie wouldn't talk about it, but Sam texted Danny and Arlen and they both showed up the next weekend.

"He creeped me out from the beginning," Rosie finally said over Friday night beers at the fire pit. "He's just a thug." She gave an involuntary shiver, remembering the debacle last Memorial Day Monday.

"So, sis, how're we gonna help you make it safe? Here you and Sam have all the crops in the ground, and the chickens have begun laying. It'd be hard to call the whole thing off, but I'm worried about you."

Arlen took a stick to play quietly with the fire. "The thing is, it's not just Jack. You said that the miners up the creek always have weapons. They'll be pissed when they find their culvert's gone missing. Could I help you get that back to where it belongs?"

Rosie looked relieved. "Arlen, that'd be a big help. Can we do that tomorrow morning before any more time passes? And could we all go together, in case they're there this weekend? Danny, will you be 'head of household' and be ready to do the talking? And I'm going to take my .38."

Sam added, "I'll take the .30-30."

Danny threw his hands up. "This isn't the Hatfields and the McCoys, Sis. It's just a case of a misunderstanding. Arlen, what do you think?"

Arlen had trained in Aikido. He had picked his martial art with some care, since the situations that led to it were not those he wanted to repeat. Acting like a tough guy had grown distasteful. As a kid, he'd been picked on and had fought back. Then he gravitated more toward things that didn't hurt — didn't hurt him, didn't hurt others.

Finally, he added his two bits to the mix. "I don't think anyone needs a gun. It may set a tone we could regret."

Rosie reacted first. "Are you saying I shouldn't protect myself? I don't get it, Arlen. Here some guy practically rapes me 'cause he thinks there's no one around, and you're saying we should go greet a bunch of guys who are armed to the teeth, with nothing ourselves?"

"Doesn't make any sense, Arlen," Sam added.

Danny equivocated. "I've never needed a gun out here," he noted, "but we took something of theirs and they could be hugely pissed."

Arlen gave it one more shot. "I just think it sends too strong a message."

The fire took one more log and they changed the topic to dredging. Danny knew the lore of the Bradshaws from the past fifty years and told a couple of miners' tales that diverted them all to regional history, part of opening the West.

In the morning, on a recount over coffee, the numbers remained the same. Guns, two; Danny, on the fence; no guns, one. They loaded their weapons, drove Arlen's pickup over the creek, up the hill to the tree line, chucked the culvert into the back of the truck, and rumbled back over the stream, down the road to where the miners had stored it for fixing a washed out pass.

In the end, weapons didn't matter. The campsite was deserted. They deposited their cargo where it had been found, ending the Great Debate between the Old-Fashioned Moralists and the New Age Relativists. The reputation of the family farm remained untainted.

Arlen and Danny exchanged cell phone numbers and agreed to spell each other so that, like it or not, Rosie would have at least one of them as a visitor through the summer. June on the farm passed swiftly with either Rosie or Sam going to Farmers Market each Saturday with a load of starts from the greenhouse and fresh organic eggs. Their new small farm was a hit and they always returned sold out.

Rosie and Sam took turns going to town during the week, and Rosie spent some time just with Arielle, processing Jack.

"I dunno, Ari, he didn't really even hurt me, but now I'm always looking around to see if someone's coming. He touched me! I don't like being this scared."

"It's natural, Rosie. That's a horrible thing to have happened. It's almost like magic that Benny showed up. Did you talk to him about it at all?"

"No. It crossed my mind that maybe he was a creep too, just arriving last at the clearing. But no, he really came in on my side. I guess he was just taking in the dawn, like I wanted to. Don't Navajos greet the sun or something?"

"I think I've heard that. I really don't know. I'm not from here. I should learn more."

"But now it's like every guy is a danger. And that's not true. Like Benny was actually a savior. And at the farm so many of the guys have been really golden — Hotchkiss, Sam, Arlen, even Chris. I know they're not bad guys, but I don't know how to act around them."

Arielle hugged her girlfriend, a long, slow embrace of sisters. "Is there something else going on? I mean, you told me about stuff when you were a kid. Do you think that has an influence on how you react now to things?"

"I don't know, Ari, I don't know. I think I'm so strong and independent, but sometimes I just blow up and sometimes I just brush the guy off. I gave Chris the cold shoulder and he's really hot. It's just that I don't want to be betrayed or dumped, and I'm sure he already has a girlfriend in town."

Ari didn't respond. Chris was a dependable friend, but he did move around among her girlfriends. He was developing something of a reputation.

"And Arlen. He's another guy who's been nothing but helpful. Unless he's gay, I don't know why he hasn't laid a hand on me. I like him, but I'm afraid to get any closer."

"Well, it seems like you have the safest bet with Sam. You've set boundaries and the two of you are just business partners, working the farm. Maybe you need some counseling, Rosie. Maybe after this summer and the fall harvest you could spend time in town and talk things out with a professional."

Ari meant well. But a wall went up inside Rosie. She was strong, independent, had it under control. She would handle it. "Thanks, girlfriend, but for now I'm just going to grow zucchini and pull weeds. If a guy wants to help that's fine. If he wants anything more, I'll give him a karate-chop."

Rosie packed up the Cherokee to return to the farm. She had seen Benny at the Market, but he didn't come over and she didn't seek him out. There was an awkward silence — not dangerous, but unsettled. She was grateful, but she sensed in Benny something older, more experienced than his age would indicate — some knowledge that held him a little distant from her and most of her Anglo friends. Maybe it was just cultural. Still, she wanted him to know. He'd save her from reliving the horrors of her childhood.

"Ari, tell Benny thanks for me. We haven't talked, but his timing was perfect. And I didn't mind the bruises from getting shoved to the ground when he tackled Jack. The black and blues were worth it. I didn't have any idea Benny could move so fast. I don't know what would have happened if he hadn't showed up when he did."

"Benny's kind of a quiet guy. Even though he doesn't talk as much as most of us white folks, he seems to know a lot about what's going on. I'll tell him you said 'thanks.' I'm sure he knows."

"When can you come visit again?"

"I'm not sure. Tony's really busy on our farm, and they're loading hours on my schedule at the café because of all the summer tourists. If I can't make it soon, I'll text. And make sure you see me when you're in town for Farmer's Market. Rosie, you are just the dearest friend I've ever had. Tony's great, but we don't talk like you and I do. I am so sorry we didn't come with you to the farm. You know how it is?" Her question wafted between them.

"You can't do it all, Ari. And Tony needs you. You and I will be friends forever. And we make great music. Let's do that next time." Rosie gave her another hug and pointed the Jeep down Main Street, off to the dirt road and Clear Creek.

With either Danny or Arlen coming up every weekend, Rosie got to like the company. There was such good warmth about Arlen, and they worked comfortably together on the yoga platform. He had beautiful crinkle lines around his warm brown eyes and an offbeat sense of humor that made her laugh. He seemed to get a kick out of her dream of someday having retreats here, even though there was no plan for it in the present. But, as for getting close, she just couldn't bring herself to let down her guard. Not now. Not with him, not with anyone. Not until … She wasn't sure what. But definitely not now.

Danny sometimes brought Hotchkiss, and the three of them would knock off at the bend in the creek where they'd set up the dredge. Or she'd tell Sam to join them and she'd tend the chickens and then wander up the meditation paths to her yoga spot. But she'd always pack her .38 in one hand and carry a wrench or hatchet in the other. Jack's ugly dust hung in the air, and she didn't feel quite the same there, alone.

When Arlen visited, the guaranteed hit was Stormy. Brutus and Bella loved romping with him in the woods, in the water, and after anything that threw off a scent. Once they all came back smelling like skunk and were banished to the outdoors.

On the theory that once a horse throws you, you've got to get back on, Arlen had proposed that they actually start work on the yoga platform Rosie had mentioned. Even Sam took some time out from the farming to lend a hand. By the end of June, they had set the pilings for a foundation. They had laid out a floor about 12 X 14 feet and had assembled frames for the sides. Next, they'd need roofing. It was more comfortable stretching out on the wooden planks than on the pebbly soil.

But her signals with Arlen were mixed. She seemed genuinely glad to see him, and they worked in harmony on the project. They'd also walk together, making more meditation paths, or picking fresh spearmint that grew in wild abundance up and down the stream. He'd sit with her up the hill where her parents' ashes lay among the leaves. The silences seemed as calm as a still pool in the stream. But there were moments when Arlen saw a distance in her eyes that allowed no one close.

Danny harbored some worries about Rosie. It wasn't so much her safety. They had the weekends covered, and the history of the place had been decades without incident. It was her stubbornness about staying there, and her overly sharp reactions to both Jack and virtually everyone else – at some point, in some conversation. As her brother, he was putting life together running the restaurant in Flagstaff. Long-term, long-distance care taking couldn't work. He felt pretty good about Sam and Arlen, but didn't feel like Sam was really in it for the long run, and Arlen was clearly rooted in the city, with the woods only a weekend pastime. This farm was not something Rosie could, or should, do all on her own.

Arlen couldn't figure her out. Couldn't figure himself out. He liked this girl. Really liked this girl. Liked her grit, liked her determination. Loved her eyes. Had a hard time looking away from her anytime. Most of the time she seemed pretty okay with him. But there was something going on that he hadn't plumbed. She kept an invisible space around her that said "No Trespassing. Remote Hideaway." It was the reaction to their regular arguments about the pump. It was the iciness surrounding Jack, a reaction that lasted larger and longer then the incident itself. It was the flare-up about the culvert and weapons. There was a sharpness with a history he didn't understand. Their food war was only the tip of the iceberg.

"Burritos?"

"Yogurt."

He wanted comfort food, she needed to control things around her. Whatever he brought in on the weekends, Sam would relish the choices. But Rosie would turn her nose up and pick through leftover lettuce rather than touch a good strip of bacon with the morning eggs. Not just different, but making a point of it every time. Food cop. But somehow, to Arlen, it didn't seem to be about food.

Summer finally arrived in Flagstaff. Wainwright limped over to the plaza to see if the afternoon drum circle had started up again. There was a familiar mix, a little smaller. College co-eds came in skirts and halter-tops to sway and stomp. He searched each face to see if the young woman with the blue eyes and dark curls would arrive in her African skirt. A longing swelled up to see her. But she never showed. Wondered if he had creeped her out. No, why should he? She didn't know him. She just liked to dance. Some part of his past was out of focus, some piece to the puzzle not coming together. He brought his drum a few times. It didn't feel quite the same.

After a few weeks Hotchkiss showed up. "Hey, Dubya, I've got it squared away with Danny. We can go to his farm on July 4 weekend. Independence Day. You can bring your .45. There will be other folks there. You up for it?"

"Sure, Hotch. I could really use a weekend away. But I don't have much dough to help with stuff."

"Not to worry. I can buy things up cheap from Kachina. Want me to pick you up at the same place?"

"Yeah." Something to look forward to.

One night at the Deportiva there was a drunken brawl. It had started with a few guys cheering for opposite baseball teams. Someone had drawn a gun. There was no time to act smooth, to settle down the ridiculously high levels of testosterone. He had sprung from around the bar and tackled the guy with the gun, sending a few others sprawling. Another patron had grabbed the gun and threw it behind the bar, where one shot blew a huge hole in the back wall. Police came, cuffed the guy, hauled him away. Thanked him for his presence of mind.

The word got around. Casey came in and talked about how it'd be good to have him on his side in a dark alley. Said he'd told Sergio and the guys. They all thought it was damn cool. And being on the right side of the law. Wasn't that a kick!

He was mainly impressed with his agility and strength.

Didn't know he had it in him to look death and danger in the eye, ignore it, and bring the guy down. Gave him an adrenaline rush. Felt damn good, in fact. Didn't realize how good a physical fight might be, with or without weapons. That night, it took a few extra beers in front of late night sports to put him to sleep.

The trip this fall. Maybe he'd wrestle a bear or something. Maybe moving huge logs out of the creek would land him a nugget big as your fist. Maybe come upon some survivalist and knock him for a loop. Possibilities were endless.

The future bore hope.

Toward the end of June, both Arlen and Danny came to the farm on the same weekend and planned a big work fiesta for the Fourth of July

"What about a barbecue?" Danny suggested. All weekend. Friday night through Monday, and folks could come up for all or part. "We could top off the yoga platform, couldn't we, Arlen? Just get the roofing on, use the battery-run drill/driver to secure the frame, and maybe slap on the sides or seal it against the weather?"

"I think we could. That what you'd like, Rosie?"

It was her project, after all. No sense in plowing ahead if she didn't buy in.

"Yes, I'd like that. And I've talked to Arielle and Professor Pete. The four of them may come out for part of the weekend, since there's an extra day."

Sam added, "I talked to Chris too. Jack is persona non grata and may have left town. Not sure. But Chris was wondering if he could bring a girl with him. Appears he's interested in her."

"Oh … Oh." Rosie was taken aback. Wasn't exactly sure how she felt about that. But she hadn't expressed any interest in him, so that's the price you pay. "Sure, tell him to bring her along. The more the merrier, and more girls will be nice too. Great… Great."

So that's that, and that's fine. Bring her along. Gives me

one less guy to be irritated at.

"So that would be six, and Hotchkiss asked me if he could bring an extra guy. Some older fellow he knows from the convenience store and drumming. A Vietnam vet. I met him once. Seems okay," Danny added. A big group on the Fourth of July weekend would be fun.

"Can you be sure to bring in enough to eat?" Sam added. "And maybe some extra beer and wine. After all, it's Independence Day, and we'll be celebrating. Maybe make a huge bonfire in the field."

Chapter 13

In Arizona, there's a joke about "monsoon season." It's not really a joke, it's just different than a monsoon in Asia. Sometimes it only amounts to a few spits of dust on your windshield. Other times the humidity turns the Valley of the Sun into an oppressive jungle. At its most exciting, huge thunder and lightening shows unleash torrents and floods to the streets and an outage of electricity to whole neighborhoods. People stand outside and meet their neighbors. Or find stray dogs. It can be dangerous and destructive. It will remind you who's boss.

Usually, the months of April, May and June are dry, and increasingly hot. They'd already seen this at the farm. They had to pump irrigation to the crops in the field and water to the chicken coop twice a week. Arlen and Rosie came to loggerheads more than once about the fitness of the motor at the well. It still limped along, but every fill-up of the uphill tank took more time.

Now, toward the end of June, you could feel the increasing humidity building up, with more high, white cumulus clouds ballooning into the cerulean summer sky. Maybe there would be some rain coming. It became a regular pattern. In the morning, day would begin clear and cloudless over the mountains. By noon there would be wisps, building to puffs in the afternoon. By sundown most of the clouds would dissipate, leaving a bright moon or thick Milky Way cutting a swath across the evening sky.

Through the end of June, and into July, every afternoon was weighed heavily with larger and larger cumulonimbus, thickening from airy and frothy white to the foggy and then heavier grays that hinted at upcoming storms.

It seemed to Arlen, as he drove out on the dirt road toward Clear Creek farm on Friday afternoon, that they might have their first big storm of the season. Forest Service signs reminded those venturing within of an alert for high fire danger. He hoped it might rain Saturday night, after the huge July 4th bonfire, just in case. Just in case. He seemed to always be packing and thinking, just in case.

The Prescott crowd also started arriving on Friday afternoon, and Chris's girlfriend Annie was a pleasant addition to the mix. Arielle knew her from the health food store. Once Rosie got over the fact that Annie was hooked up with Chris, she warmed up and welcomed her like an old friend. Chris could remain Rosie's friend, and Annie and she and Arielle could make music. Pete and Chloe had made amends after Rosie's tongue-lashing over the theft. They became more protective following the episode with Jack. The regulars had become a pretty convivial group of friends, supporting the sustainable agriculture idea with a fun escape on the weekends after too much drudgery in town.

They spent most of Friday evening cleaning eggs and picking veggies so that Sam could do the stint at Farmers Market Saturday. He was up and out by five in the morning.

On Saturday, Danny arrived about ten in the morning, and following him was Hotchkiss in a separate pickup truck. When Hotchkiss's friend got out of the passenger side, Rosie froze up. What the heck? This was the old guy at the African dance class whose eyes seemed to bore through her. Now she realized. Even though the guy was over sixty, he reminded her of *him*. Same dark hair. Same tall, skinny frame. No wonder the guy made her shudder. The guy hunched over like *he* had hunched over her. It was not *him*, but he stirred the deep, horrible fear she still felt from before. Felt it again, fully, for the first time in years. Internally, a wave of revulsion reverberated within her body. On the surface, she tried to look normal.

"Hi, Rosie," Hotchkiss began, giving her a light hug. "This is my friend Wainwright, from town, but I call him 'Dubya.' He's okay with that, aren't you, Dubya?"

Wainwright started to say, "Pleased to meet you," but he stopped in his tracks. Wait a minute! This was the girl in the African dance class. Recovering, he mustered some manners. "Say, haven't I seen you before? Don't mean to be rude, but weren't you in Flagstaff at some African dance class?"

Danny put two and two together. "Yeah, Hotchkiss, I remember you talking about that. Rosie, remember how I mentioned some guys came over once or twice to jam? Dubya was one of them. And Dubya, Rosie stayed with me the night that Josuf Mbwana was instructing a class. She was wiped out that night. Remember how you were so exhausted, Rosie?"

Rosie collected herself and held out a hand. "Hello, Mr. Dubya," she said cautiously. She instinctively stayed near Arlen.

Arlen felt the awkwardness permeating the air. This was strange — a coincidence, but not entirely a good feeling about it from Rosie. What was going on?

Danny changed the pace by suggesting that anyone who was interested follow him up the hill to help Arlen work on the Yoga House, which was now its official name.

As the day progressed, the platform was completed, the framed sides were raised, and the roof was secured, making a successful ramada, or shelter from the sun.

Arlen noticed a pattern. Just about everyone pitched in, at least for a while, except Wainwright. Then they would go off in pairs, either to try out the meditation paths, splash in the creek, or disappear into the trees. Since arriving in Arizona, he hadn't had a girlfriend. He watched as Tony and Ari, Chris and Annie, and even Pete and Chloe headed off in separate pairs, a blanket in tow, for what was obviously a tryst in the forest. He became aroused thinking he might someday walk down the creek with Rosie, bedroll in hand. He longed to make love to her, tenderly, lovingly, in the sunshine or under the stars. He imagined caressing all the curves of her body, her hair tossed back, as he kissed her on her eyelashes, her cheeks, her mouth...

But this was way ahead of its time. He needed to shove those fantasies out of his head. He diverted his thoughts to the dogs as they gamboled in and out of earshot.

Wainwright stayed with the construction crew. He smoked one cigarette after the other, stomping butts out in the dirt. He didn't lift a clipper, but he talked a blue streak, about other camping trips, about how he'd been a helicopter pilot in Vietnam, how he'd been a sharpshooter, about his Purple Heart and Distinguished Service Medal, how he had an arsenal of weapons and knew how to use them. He limped down the hill only once, to replenish his personal beer supply. By lunch he'd downed a six-pack. And he seemed constantly focused on Rosie. Danny noticed it too and asked Hotchkiss what was up.

"He's a vet, y'know, down on his luck." Hotchkiss guessed. "I'd say he has PTSD. Lotta talk, but not too coherent."

Danny and Hotchkiss decided to stay on him. In the afternoon they took Wainwright off to dredge for gold. Most everyone either took a siesta. Chloe and Pete again strolled downstream again an afternoon *rendez-vous* at their private waterfall. Chris and Annie seemed to have similar thoughts, heading upstream with their bedroll. They returned with straw-messed hair, Annie looking sheepish.

Twice in the same day! Rosie couldn't help but notice Chloe's unbuttoned shorts and Annie's blush. Just wondering about them all, she felt a wave of arousal surge through her. But it was a desire choked by fear. Would she ever feel safe enough to do it, to love a man, to make love, to have sex like everyone around her? Would it help to just surrender to lust with the nearest available male body?

Not after Jack. Even his filthy hands had started to arouse in her a feeling of being in rut. The rapidity of arousal, even at the hands of someone who she despised, brought up feelings of guilt and shame. It disgusted and frightened her.

Somehow, somewhere she'd have to free herself from this feeling of filth connected to sex. She'd have to find a way to be — well — normal. And she'd have to find a man she could trust. A man who could be gentle and patient as he brought her slowly, safely, into a place of sexual pleasure.

In the afternoon, the clouds did another buildup, more leaden than before, casting immense shadows across the field. People started to gather on the wide veranda-porch that encircled the house.

When Sam returned from the market, he'd had another sellout. Benny Whitehorse, who'd had to put in some intern time in the emergency room at Yavapai Regional Medical Center, came with him. Benny had brought some graham crackers, chocolate and marshmallows for s'mores over the evening fire.

"Hi, Benny." Rosie was the first to welcome him, after congratulating Sam on the sales. "Glad you could make it. Thanks for ... you know."

Couldn't be there for my little sister. "That's okay. Glad I was there at the right time." Benny tossed it off as not a big deal. But they both knew it was.

They grilled burgers and dogs and toasted their buns on the grill over the fire pit. The food, beer and wine fostered a spirit of general conviviality. After dinner, Sam and Chris built the fire up high and Chloe broke out a bunch of bottle-rockets and sparklers.

Rosie tried to avoid Wainwright, but he kept approaching, and said more than twice, "I feel like I knew you from somewhere else, Rosie. You sure we haven't met before?"

Hotchkiss, Danny and Arlen rotated shifts at her side. Danny and Hotchkiss then rotated shifts at Dubya's side too, because he was again too much into the sauce.

After dinner, Danny brought out his guitar, and Rosie's,

and Hotchkiss added a set of hand drums. They meandered through the Eagles, James Taylor, Grateful Dead, Hank Williams–an eclectic group to suit everyone's tastes. Hotchkiss and Wainwright took turns on the drums. After awhile, someone doused the fire.

Though neither one paid attention to the other, both Rosie and Wainwright took solace in the rhythm of the drums, taking them away from their memories, giving them momentary safety and relief in the music.

Above them, in the night air, the clouds thinned. It guaranteed a starry night, but the high wisps were a harbinger that storms were still in the forecast. Several people took their sleeping bags off the porch and slept under the sky.

Wainwright awoke in the morning, stiff and hung over. He had slept badly – again. He could blame it on the dog hair in the sleeping bag, chips from the stacked firewood, or even the beer. But in truth, it was the nightmare of the crash, when the helicopter went down. He was helpless to prevent disaster while his best friend was incinerated and he, Wainwright, was thrown, injured but safe. The flashbacks kept returning. What made matters worse this weekend was that the crash had happened on Independence Day, decades ago in a country far away from home. This was a horrible anniversary.

Even if he got up and drank some coffee, even then the nightmare would stay behind his eyelids. It wouldn't rest. But he rolled out of his bag and walked out back to take a whiz against some locust bushes.

Rosie called from the propane stove, "If anyone wants coffee you'll have to come get it."

"Thanks," he said. "Thanks, young lady. You sure are nice to make coffee for everyone. Thanks. I thank you. Did I ever tell you...?"

"If you want to talk, you'll have to follow me up the hill while I let out the chickens. I don't have time to stop and chat."

"Sure, sure."

But Sam was already joining her down the steps and up the driveway to the coop. Wainwright plopped on the porch bench next to the plastic cooler and popped the top off a beer.

"Gotta chase that coffee with something," he muttered to Bella, who came up to sniff both drinks.

He watched Rosie striding up the road toward the chickens when suddenly it hit him. She was almost the spitting image of his wife Jean, the woman he had loved so much before the war and whom he drove to divorce upon his return over thirty years ago. The short curly hair was different than Jean's braid, but the size, the eyes, the gait, the determination – they were the same.

He hadn't been able to tell Jean about the nightmares. Marines didn't complain — they were warriors, they stuffed it. And the only legitimate form of self-medication was booze and cigarettes. So he hooked himself on Camels and whiskey, took out his chaos on Jean, and she left. Lord, he'd missed her all these years. Never had another woman. Just gave up. Gave in to the turmoil inside his head.

Jean had left and taken all their photographs. He'd struggled to recall her image, but it had eluded him since she left. Until now. But here was this lovely young lady at this beautiful farm. If he and Jean had ever had a daughter, she would have looked just like Rosie. Of that he became absolutely sure.

Chris and Annie whipped up a pile of pancakes, and Arlen provided a side of bacon that made everyone happy. Except Rosie.

"There you go, Arlen," she chided. "Just can't stay away from shooting cholesterol, can you?"

"Oh, come on now," Danny said. "We've all worked hard, and we're in the woods. Jeez, Rosie, give the man a break. We deserve this delicious, fatty, greasy, smoked piece of heaven. Agreed?"

There was a round of applause on that one, and Rosie shut up. But she glared at Danny. *You know I hate to be shown up in public, brother. I'll find a way to get back at you.*

The clouds built up rapidly Sunday morning, and the sky darkened. Rosie was glad they'd put sealant on the Yoga House floor and sides yesterday. The pinewood planks would stay dry if the monsoon hit.

Most of the work was complete, so Sam and Danny started talking guns. "I like the Glock," Sam claimed.

Spontaneously, he picked up the firearm, took it in both hands, adopted the stance, and shot off the porch at the liter plastic bottles strung like laundry between two trees standing 60 feet away. The first shot missed, the second hit its mark. There was modest applause, showing a division between the Second Amendment fans and Gun Control advocates parked on the veranda.

But Sam had broken the unspoken rule – no target practice from the porch when people were visiting.

Danny was about to remind folks that they should move down the meadow for any gun use when he noticed Wainwright swinging a .45 pistol in his right hand, a beer in his left.

"I was a sharpshooter in the war," Dubya was saying. "I could hit anything from a moving position." His stories were not matching up. He couldn't be both pilot and sharpshooter. Hotchkiss started to wonder. Dubya kept right on: "We'd sweep the site for the enemy, we'd …"

Arlen stared at him. Whether Wainwright realized it or not, his thumb, clumsy with either booze or arthritis, had slipped off the side safety. A squeeze on the back of the handle, combined with a squeeze of the trigger could …

He spoke urgently but softly. "Hey, Dubya, makes me a little nervous, you and the gun and the beer, with so many of us on the porch. Think you could put the .45 down until later, maybe go out in the field for some target practice?"

"Didn't bother you when Sam shot off a round," Wainwright retorted, slurring his words. "I don't see no problem. I know what I can …"

He swung the pistol around sloppily as if trying to make a point. But suddenly, his finger squeezed the trigger and a shot went off the porch. Whether he had taken aim at anything they'd never know, because the bullet sailed into the driveway right by the dogs and creased Brutus on the hip. A sustained howl went up as the dog jumped, then fell, cringing and moaning, on the ground. Nina and Stormy started barking and howling. Blood gushed from the Lab's wound.

"Good God, Dubya, what've you done?" Hotchkiss seized the weapon in a flash. Danny took the beer.

Without a thought, Benny ran off the porch, grabbed his first-aid kit from Sam's truck, and tended to Brutus. He squeezed out some antibiotic salve and pressed his shirt against the dog's thigh to stanch the flow of blood.

Stormy and Bella barked in frantic chorus, so Rosie and Arlen held them down, trying to soothe them back to quiet.

"I... I... I..." Wainwright was struck dumb. Never in his whole life had he hurt an animal, and never had he fired a shot without complete control. He had never let loose the safety. Here he had come to this exquisite place, found the girl who could be his daughter, and practically killed her dog. He collapsed heavily on the porch steps, his face in his hands.

Benny spoke first. "Brutus will need a vet fast. I could find one in Prescott ..."

"I'll take him," Arlen replied. "Stormy and Brutus are pals. It's just a bit longer trip to Phoenix, but I can put Stormy in the back seat and Brutus in front. I know a vet in town who takes weekend calls. Benny, do you have a sedative? Rosie, is this okay with you? Can you keep Bella here alone?"

Rosie was still holding Bella. She watched Benny calm Brutus with one hand while digging out some clean gauze from his kit with the other. She studied the scene quickly. Benny could probably help, but there was something intuitively safe about Arlen handling Brutus. He'd saved Stormy. She could keep Bella at the farm.

"Yes, that'd work." Then she looked at Danny pleadingly. "Can you take Mr. Dubya out of here, fast?"

Danny and Hotchkiss both agreed to leave for Flagstaff, tag teaming, Wainwright riding with Hotchkiss. The old man had voluntarily surrendered his weapon and appeared to be in a state of shock. They let him sit on the steps while they packed, took coffee for three, then left.

"I'll call you soon, sis," Danny said as he hugged her good-bye.

How many crises would there be? How long could she stay here? Sure, it was the middle of summer, and they had a full harvest ahead of them. But he left the place uneasy about the sister he knew, loved, and who seemed to be a trouble magnet.

Rosie held Bella and stroked Brutus while Benny wrapped the wound. Brutus would be away from the farm for weeks. Arlen rose and helped Sam put the weapons back in the house on their respective racks, safeties all in place, unloaded, and closed up the ammo. Then he stood with a mug of coffee, catching his breath. The Prescott bunch attended to dishes, generally straightened up, brewed another pot of coffee, brought tools in from the field, and quietly rehashed the incident. Adrenaline levels receded slowly.

Finally, Rosie relinquished Brutus to Arlen's care. Wordlessly, he and Benny wrapped Brutus in a blanket. Benny gently grabbed a clump of furry shoulder between thumb and fingers in his left hand and pressed the needle into the flesh with his right. Brutus would be out for the count on the drive down the mountain to the valley. Stormy hopped into the cramped back seat so his friend could rest in front.

Rosie offered Arlen a quick hug. "Thanks. Call me. I'll come to town if you can't bring him back."

"Let's just see. I'll call and let you know what the vet says. I'm guessing at least two weeks of quiet recoup time before he lets him come back to the farm." Arlen let his arm rest around her shoulders. She remained still. In the heat of the commotion, his arm around her felt safe. Like Brutus would be as they went down the Black Mesa highway toward Phoenix. She felt her cheeks flush. *Please, no one notice.* Arlen was opening the door on the driver's side. He slid in, started the engine, and took off.

The clouds had been building up the whole morning, and as Arlen's truck rumbled into the distance, the rains began. First in misty drops, then in huge globs, finally in wind-driven sheets across the meadow. They stood somberly on the porch, absorbing the cool wetness, weighing the import of the near-tragedy, and gratefully allowing the first monsoon storm to assuage their emotions.

After the weekend of the Fourth, the summer settled in with heat, rain, and the sheer drudgery of farming. The chickens had to be fed twice daily and their eggs collected and cleaned. The vegetables had to be weeded and harvested as close to Market as possible. Friday nights Rosie and Sam would work into the evening, cleaning and packing eggs. Saturday morning they would arise in the darkness, headlamps their only light, to pick vegetables at their freshest. They'd arrive before 5:30 at the Farmers Market in town. Their sales were brisk and successful. Sometimes, they wanted to stay in town for an occasional party, but if they drove only one truck they had to return after the market. The chickens had to be fed. They would arrive home late Saturday evening, exhausted, and sleep most of Sunday.

With the coming of monsoon rains, the creek began to swell and rise. Although they had rigged a black plastic bag to catch the heat and a sprinkler head for warm showers, Rosie and Sam often took to the deep dredging-holes, often five feet deep, to clean themselves off.

One afternoon, after a long stretch of fence repairs, they headed upstream. They shed their sweaty clothes and lowered themselves, completely naked, into a pool.

Rosie and Sam knew each other's bodies. Working the fields, dropping dirty and sweaty clothes at the end of the day, either one might strip completely, streaked with sweat and dirt, to sponge off or dip in the creek. More than once, they'd run outside nude to frolic in the monsoon storms. They had looked each other over, but the boundaries were set. Rosie kept it that way. If it bothered Sam, he didn't let it show. His first goal was to make the farm work. So they settled into an intimate, but non-sexual, friendship, almost like brother and sister. Sam caught the flu after one rainy day at Market. Rosie bathed his skinny hairy body to cool him down. Rosie got terrible cramps before her period. Sam would heat a water bottle and place it, wrapped in a towel, on her bare abdomen.

"Say, Rosie, I've been thinking. I'd like to invite Benny out again and have him help us make a sweat lodge. Don't Navajos do that?"

"Yeah they do, but what for?"

"I've heard you get really clean. They put hot rocks into the center of the lodge (a hut, really), and pour water over, and the temperature gets you so hot you just sweat all the gunk out of your system. Then you head for the creek and plunge in, even if it's cold – especially if it's cold. The cold water closes up your pores and you stay cleaner. Or at least, so I've heard."

"Yeah, not something we've been able to do here this summer. Sometimes at Market I wonder if we smell weird to the customers. I hope the table between me and them keeps them clueless about how unwashed I can sometimes be." Rosie dipped under the water and soaked her hair, rising with it flowing behind her face.

"So, you like the idea ok? I can ask him out after I do a Saturday market. You could stay home, we come back Saturday night, work all Sunday, I take him back to town Monday and do a quick hardware shop. That'd work."

"Aren't sweat lodges more of a spiritual thing? I mean, yeah, you can have a steam or sauna to clean the pores, but aren't you supposed to purge the demons or get insight, Sam? I thought that's what I'd heard."

"Maybe. I'll ask Benny. But either way, it wouldn't hurt. Be kind of interesting. Maybe he could help me build a teepee too. I've got the poles from fallen Alder tree trunks. That's really be fun."

"Navajos don't have teepees. That's Midwestern." Rosie felt downright scholarly next to this guy from the east. "But we could do it together if Benny didn't want to. No rule against an Anglo teepee, is there?"

Sam ducked under, running his hands through his hair to dislodge any big dirt chunks. He came up with a smile.

"Who'd catch us anyway out here at the farm? Let's do it."

So the following weekend, Sam went to Market and the two guys came back. There wasn't much talk. The work was making her and Sam bone-tired, and Benny was just downright quiet. But on Sunday morning, Sam initiated the conversation over breakfast.

"So, Benny, how do we do this? Are there rules for building a sweat lodge? It sounds so cool."

Benny, uncharacteristically, studied Sam's face. Then he looked at Rosie with such calm that she looked away, uncomfortable.

"Sam, I am doing this for Rosie. A sweat can be just for physical cleansing. That's what you mentioned at Farmer's Market. But the more important part of a sweat is in its history and intent. It is not just a building. It is a ceremony. Its purpose is a healing purpose. If that's ok with each of you, I'll help you build one."

"Sure," Sam said, eagerly.

Rosie felt something turn over inside her. Like a movement from despair toward hope. It was a much larger reaction than she expected. "Benny, you're really asking something serious, aren't you?"

"Yes, I am."

"I'd be honored if you'd help us. I don't feel quite worthy…"

"We can build it today, Rosie. And when the time comes, we can have the ceremony. I'll show you how."

They spent the rest of the morning building the sweat lodge. First, they walked around the outside fire pit across the creek. The fire pit would be necessary to heat the large stones that would be placed in the lodge during the sweat. The land to the west was grassy and flat, close to a stone wall. The opening would face east – toward the fire pit, toward the creek, and toward the rising sun.

"Do you think there would be more than four of you, or us, in a sweat at any one time?" Benny asked. "That will affect the size."

"No, I can't imagine everyone here wanting to do it. Three or four – that sounds about right."

They dug a small hole that they would later make into the pit for hot rocks that would mark the center of the lodge. Then they marked off with their feet a circle with a diameter of about eight feet. That would allow for about four people, sitting cross-legged, to sit in a circle around the pit, facing each other.

Sam and Benny dug a dozen holes for the saplings that would form the frame of the hut. Rosie gathered several young oaks, already curved as they sprung from the root of their parent tree. The poles had to be curved or pliable, to bend to the shape of a dome. The three of them set the poles in the ground, almost a foot deep, and packed the dirt around them to keep them from being dislodged. Then they used twine to latch the saplings together. When they had finished, the poles formed a circular dome about five feet tall at the center. The next step was to cover the dome with tarps and blankets, leaving one area facing the fire pit open as an entrance. It would have a flap to cover it once all the rocks and participants were inside, ready to begin. Other than the flap, there would be no heat or light coming into or leaving the hut.

El Nino had been blowing heavy moisture up from the south, and just as they lashed the last few poles together, it began to rain. There was little warning. Soon the rain poured. Sam, Benny and Rosie ran, soaked, to the veranda.

"It looks great to me," Sam said, admiring his own efforts.

"It is good. It will be sturdy." Benny simply looked at their handiwork. "But today is not the day for a sweat. Can't do it in the rain. Besides," he glanced at Rosie, "it isn't quite time. And I have to get back to town. I have the early shift tomorrow morning."

So, after changing to dry clothes and having a lunch of hot soup, Rosie drove Benny back into Prescott.

They said very little along the way. Each seemed to guard his or her own thoughts. Eventually Rosie asked, "You said it isn't quite time for a sweat. What did you mean, Benny?"

The Navajo remained quiet for a very long time. Rosie began to think he hadn't heard her. Finally he said, "People need to feel ready to enter into the hut for the sweat. It is very hot, very close. The body changes. The Great Spirit must give his blessing. It is very spiritual, Rosie."

They pulled up to Benny's place and he slung his leather satchel over his shoulder, ready to hop out of the Jeep. "Will I see you soon, then?" Rosie asked.

"I'm not quite sure. I'm pretty busy with summer school finals. That wraps up EMT school for me. Work starts in the fall. I don't know what my time will look like. But the sweat will happen. You will know when the time is right. And I will come and help you with your ceremony." He gave a slight, shy nod, and got out of the car, jogging through the rain to his house.

Rosie spent the night with Ari. Tony had to do some swap work for a few days on a friend's farm, so the girls had a night to themselves. Rosie described the making of the lodge frame with Benny, and what he'd said about 'the right time.'

"Do you think he likes you, Rosie, I mean *likes* you, you know, in a romantic way? I've seen him be pretty attentive to you. I know there are cultural issues, but he seems pretty attached to Prescott. And I've never seen him give as much attention to anyone as he does to you." Ari strummed some background chords as she spoke.

"Wow! You know, I never picked up a vibe like that, Ari. But then, I'm not one to tell anyway. I'm so retarded when it comes to romance, to sex, to men. But no, I don't think so. I don't know what it is. But it's different. He's different. After the thing with Jack, I feel like he knows something. He seems – well, wiser than most guys his age." Rosie took her guitar out and matched chords with Ari.

"I don't know, Rosie," Ari faltered. I mean, we've known each other a long time and gone through some deep stuff together. You've talked about your past, and then the year when your parents were killed. You've had a lot of trauma. Would you ever think, after the harvest, of coming into town and maybe seeing a counselor? Like, someone professional?"

"Let's just sing, ok? I don't want to talk about stuff like that. I can handle it. Let's hit some of the old lullabyes. That'll be a good way to get to sleep."

Friends came out for the weekend less often. The grind of it all wasn't much fun, and neither were Rosie and Sam. They lost track of the weeks, and late summer slipped into autumn.

Rosie thought a lot of Arlen, and his comfort and humor, but she put him out of her mind. He had brought Brutus back after three weeks, in late July, but their time together was brief. She put up a barrier against his warmth and he knew it.

She thought, too, about Benny and Jack. Benny, someone she hardly knew, had appeared at just the right moment and saved her from an attempted rape. How had he known?

The incident with Jack still stuck in her throat, bad enough in itself but a trigger to flashbacks about her childhood, the "haunted house," to *him*. Sometimes she would still awake in the midst of a nightmare, the recurrent dream of being trapped, the fear of rape, the fear of death. She tried to rationalize it away. "I hate you, I want you dead," she'd whisper under her breath to the window, as if *he* might hear, as if her whisper could kill.

Then she'd drift towards Mom and Dad. "Where were you? Why didn't you protect me? I needed you! I was so little, so helpless." And then the overwhelming grief that they were irrevocably dead, taken from her, as if abandoning her twice, without her having any say over any of it.

To suppress the thoughts that haunted her daily, she threw all her energy into the farm. Weeding, fence repair, egg collecting, freshening the coop with new hay. Every task, like African dance, took on a methodical, persistent rhythm, drumming images of beans and zucchini into her struggling psyche.

She didn't talk about it with Sam. Talking with Danny had been painful enough, but at least Danny was part of it. He understood. He'd been a victim too. No, she didn't want to divulge the torment of her childhood. She was determined not to define herself – not to let herself be defined – by the past. She was in the here and now. That's the Rosie the world would know.

Besides, she owed it to Sam. They'd both put in money, both taken a risk, both invested themselves fully in making the farm work. She and Sam had to make a return on this investment, prove it to everyone, to themselves.

The dirt under her fingernails and the sweaty grime on her body no longer washed away. The solar shower hooked up outside the house worked through September. By October, it ran out of warmth before it ran out of water. Suds became a luxury. You could wash them off shivering or forego soap entirely. As the days shortened, headlamps stayed on longer as they picked the last few harvests and packed them for market.

Arlen let over a month go by. Work was busy, and he really had mixed feelings. They had been through some stuff together, shared their pasts, felt synchronized in constructing the Yoga House. He'd loved seeing that become a reality for her, as it seemed to be her secret heart's desire. But when he brought Brutus back after the accident, pretty well healed but for a slight limp, she was distant, even asking him to baby-sit the farm while she and Sam went in to market. He left early that August Sunday and hadn't called since.

The receptionist at Coconino Counseling Services studied the grimy referral slip. The 90-day expiration date was today. "You just made it under the wire, mister. What took you so long?" But she shouldn't have asked. The old guy's desperation provided the answer.

"I called. I have an appointment." Wainwright leaned both hands on the desk, as if seeking the appointment book for reassurance. "Wainwright, Alden Wainwright."

"Oh, yes, here it is," the lady muttered, embarrassed by her gaffe. "Dr. Thorne will be with you in just a few moments." Thorne read the file. The referral had come from the VA. There seemed to be a constant stream of them these days: Vietnam, Beirut, Gulf, Iraq, Afghanistan. Depression, anxiety, nervousness, maybe nerve disorders, panic, and what seemed to be a lot of PTSD–post-traumatic stress disorder.

The DSM IV – *Diagnostic and Statistical Manual of Mental Disorders* — a "bible" in the mental health profession — had clarified some of these conditions, especially PTSD. Thorne guessed that a lot of men in previous wars had suffered the same conditions when it didn't have a name. "Shell shock," some had called it, after World War II. But PTSD made its home in the lexicon of mental health issues toward the end of the Vietnam War. Its diagnosis had become more precise, and new treatment models had emerged.

"Mr. Wainwright, I'm Jonathon Thorne. C'mon in."

Wainwright entered the room, reassured by the soft lighting, and sat in what, in his anxiety and anticipation, he had named "the hot seat."

"I almost killed a dog," Wainwright blurted out. "I love animals, and I shot the poor critter. I would never in my right mind ..." He held his head in his hands, then wiped his runny nose with a dirty rag.

Thorne handed him a box of fresh tissues. "Well, Mr. Wainwright, or do you have another name you like to be called?"

Didn't feel like Thorne was trying to shame or threaten. Good. He was scared enough.

"Yeah, my name is Alden, but my pals call me Dubya. Funny, I thought that president was a dumb prick, but the name kinda grew on me. And maybe I'm a dumb prick too."

"Dubya. Dubya." Thorne let the diphthong wash aurally around. "Sure it's okay?"

"Yeah, it's okay. I think Rosie'd think it's okay."

Rosie. Hmm. Thorne wondered who that was. "So, if you're ready, let's begin. It's not just about the dog, is it?"

Late September. Days growing shorter. He gave notice at Club Deportiva that he'd be taking a weekend off in October. Told the boss about target practice, panning for gold, going hunting with Sergio and the guys. He'd bought out Wal-Mart the day ammo came in for his .22.

Just a week or so to go. The summer had been long and hot. He was up for some action.

Chapter 14

By late September, Arlen simply missed her. So he called.

"Rosie, I haven't heard from you in awhile. Stormy and I were wondering if you'd like visitors. I can help pack the truck and feed the hens."

His voice at the other end stirred up the anxiety again. Why this unease around Arlen? He'd been nothing but a gentleman. He'd helped her with the yoga deck. He'd worked on the pump. He'd taken Brutus to the vet after that disaster with Wainwright.

But he was a man, and despite all the appearances of having a lot of guys around and all the work that seemed to require help from them, Rosie was scared. Arlen was likeable. That's what was wrong with him.

"Well, all we're doing is working hard to get stuff to market. You'd be bored."

Rosie knew that was a lame excuse, and Arlen guessed right that she didn't really mean it. She and Sam got on each other's nerves, and the farm could get lonely. So he pushed the envelope a little.

"Not to worry. I'll work on that beloved pump of yours and see if I can get it to work once and for all. Okay?"

Arlen arrived Friday evening at dusk. It was early October, the fall equinox had come and gone, and the days had shortened. As promised, he brought a thick piece of tenderloin that they threw on the outside grill. Fresh greens and potatoes from the field rounded out a fine dinner. They packed the truck with the cage-free eggs.

Before dawn, when they usually rose to pick the vegetables, Sam offered, "Say, why don't you two stay here today? I can handle Market myself. You've been a big help packing the truck. I have some errands and want to stay in town overnight. Tony and Arielle may have a barbecue later, and it would feel good to hang with them for a bit."

"So you get a break from the farm, is that it?"

Rosie teased him but realized that the deal could help her too. Market was grueling work, and she could really use time away from Sam. They weren't lovers, just business partners, and he had some irritating habits that grated on her.

"Okay," she conceded, "but how about you get a few things on my list, and we'll take care of the chickens for you."

So, by five in the morning, Sam was rumbling down the road. Arlen lingered on the porch steps. "It's so quiet, and still early in the day. Why don't we take a walk along the creek? Then we can come back and catch a nap or get breakfast a little later."

They headed gradually upstream. As the sky started to pale, the first birds awoke with a fluttering chatter. Arlen followed Rosie as she picked her way among the locust bushes between the rocks.

He tapped her shoulder. "Over there," he whispered.

A mother deer and young fawn, still spotted and delicate, stood upstream, drinking at the water's edge. They remained still for several seconds. Then the deer caught a scent in the morning mist and looked their way. Rosie and Arlen stood perfectly still, staring back. After a long minute's gaze, the mother finally nudged her youngster. They turned and disappeared through the bushes into the forest.

"That was magical," Rosie whispered.

Arlen nodded. "Very lucky to be so close,"

He rested a hand on her shoulder. Maybe she'd soften a little, not seem so scared, so put-offish.

Rosie shuddered inwardly. Why? Why Arlen? She let his hand stay. Suddenly a bevy of wild turkeys emerged from a stand of maple and oak, crunching the fallen leaves as they scurried to pass away from these humans.

Arlen smiled. "They seem to be in a hurry. Lucky for them it's not hunting season."

He took his arm off her shoulder and hunched down to cup his hands for a sip of clear water.

Rosie felt the spot on her shoulder cool, where his hand had made it warm. "We might as well get back," she said with some regret. "I could use some coffee this morning, and it takes awhile for the stove to make it perk."

On their return trip, they picked a stand of wild spearmint. Rosie would later dry it for a soothing tea. Then they discovered a patch of wild strawberries. Small but juicy, the berries complemented a fruit bowl at breakfast.

"Pick a project you really want to accomplish today, Rosie, and I'll help you get it done." Arlen let her pass in front of him as they went into the house.

Over heirloom eggs and fresh cinnamon rolls, they revisited their encounters upstream. And, by the way, how did Arlen know she loved cinnamon rolls? Licking the extra icing off the aluminum tray, she realized that she really appreciated the thoughtful foodie touches he brought when he came. Not the chorizo and bacon, but the tenderloin and occasional sweets. He noticed the little details.

"I don't think I could live here full time," Arlen mused, "but it's so peaceful. You must have loved coming here with your mom and dad."

Rosie was startled to hear him mention her parents. Actually, he knew more about the pump and her father than anyone else, maybe even Danny. Somehow, Arlen's honoring the time they had given her was comforting, like keeping a memory alive but without the pain she felt when she had carried the knowledge alone.

"You know what I'd really like to do? I've been working on my little meditation paths, as they do switchbacks and zigzags up the hill to the platform in the clearing. I'd love to have at least one path cleared all the way around the hill. You willing to try that?"

"Con gusto, amiga," Arlen replied.

There was a lot of Spanish spoken in Phoenix, and he'd picked up this Latino expression from Adriana. It required no translation.

With the dogs bounding around them, sniffing under bushes, disappearing into the underbrush, Arlen and Rosie spent several hours in the morning creating and smoothing trails. Arlen used a rock bar to wedge out the smaller rocks and a hoe to make the path about two feet wide. Rosie lopped off branches that interfered with human traffic. Often they'd use fallen branches or rocks to make an edge so that newcomers could easily find their way, even after a light snow might fall upon the trail.

Around noon, they met their goal of bringing one of the zags all the way around the hill and back to the clearing. Resting on the edge of the platform, chugging from a canteen, they looked out over the pine-covered slopes, each with private thoughts. When the sun was high in the southern sky, they headed back to the house to make lunch. Afterward, a short nap on the veranda restored them from their earlier sleep loss.

"I think it's time I checked on the hens and gathered the next round of eggs," Rosie announced, to convince herself she was really getting up.

"I'll do what I promised, and that's to take another look at your motor at the well," Arlen replied. "But I really think it's on its last legs. It's had a long run. I'll try to keep it going, but ..."

"Well, I'm counting on you to make it work. We've got to make it through October."

Having run wild up the creek all morning, the dogs lay sacked out in the living room. The humans set off alone to pursue their separate tasks.

Fall nipped the air. The oak leaves reddened, the walnut leaves turned gold. Dark branches and evergreens etched the clear blue sky

She had just finished giving the hens their water and feed, thrown in some hay, and locked the gate, when she saw five men approaching up the drive.

At first, she couldn't make them out. Men? Why men today? Why five? Then, as they came closer, she realized with panic that they all carried guns. Three held rifles, two had pistols in their hands.

And one of the five was *him*.

One of them spoke. "Hey, there's that cute little chick you told us about. I thought she was in California."

"Yeah, what's she doing here?" another asked.

And the third one said, "No matter, she's alone. Well, now, ain't that convenient?"

Rosie stood dumbstruck, frozen with fear. Not *him*, not *him* again! She'd forgotten her .38. She looked around in desperation and found nothing.

"What are you doing here?" She tried to sound her toughest, spitting steel edges into each word.

"Well, you were supposed to be in California..." he started to say.

She found herself breaking in. "This is *our* place, my *parent's* place. It's not yours. *You* don't belong here. *You* have no right to be here!" The pitch of her voice rose inside her skull.

"Hey, guys, she's an easy target. There are five of us, and one of her. What are we waiting for?" One of them started to move toward Rosie.

He seemed to be waiting for something. And, as Rosie stared at him, she realized he wasn't as big as she thought. Skinny, yes, but shorter than Wainwright by several inches.

"You aren't supposed to be here..." He started again. He could feel the old anger welling up in him, adrenalin starting to pump. Like the night of the brawl at the bar.

She screamed this time. "Shut up!" Panic rose in her throat.

Casey egged him on. "You can take her. Just like at the bar. Go for it, fella. She's an easy target."

They hadn't heard Arlen approach behind them from the well. "Hello, can I help you?" he asked. Arlen's question was really a statement. It was more than a statement. It was a very measured statement that he was *here*.

He started to yell at Rosie, "Who the hell is he?"

"I'm Arlen. Who are you?"

No answer. Instead, one of the other guys said, "We were just hiking through. Doing a little target practice. Thinking of panning for gold. Maybe hunting. We're armed, in case you didn't notice."

"Yes. Everyone in the forest has guns. Anything special we should know about yours?"

Arlen put an arm around Rosie. There was something heightened, a history here. The smell of danger was palpable.

Sergio held his gun in one hand and lunged at Arlen, aiming the rifle butt as a club. Arlen moved so quickly Rosie didn't see the shift of legs, of balance. He stepped lightly aside, parried the gun butt with the backside of his hand, and swept Sergio's legs with one of his own. Sergio fell from his own force in a heap on the ground. Arlen turned to face the others.

Suddenly, the other four raised their weapons toward Arlen and Rosie. Arlen raised his hands from the elbow, palms front, facing them unarmed.

"Look, I'm not sure what you all are doing here. But you are trespassing on this lady's property. We don't make a point of carrying weapons, and the woods are generally quite safe for humans." He glanced at the pistols, then the rifles. "Not so safe for deer. But as you must have noticed, this property is marked both as to no trespassing and as a wildlife refuge. No hunting here."

Having Arlen next to her was like having the drummers at the dance. His presence provided a rhythm to steady her wildly beating heart. He was helping her keep her feet on the ground, keep herself rooted in the present.

"Arlen," she said, never taking her eyes off the short lanky one with the dark hair and eyes, "I never told you about *him*. But I need to say something."

Arlen paused. He studied the five men, and *that one* in particular. The one who looked like a younger, smaller version of Dubya? The guy he had deflected scurried back to the group. Nothing else outstanding or unusual about them, except that they were armed, guns pointed at Rosie and him, they were on her land, and there was no one but these five men, himself, and Rosie, unarmed. Never taking his eyes off them, not moving quickly, not lowering his hands, Arlen spoke.

"Why don't you say what you need to say, Rosie?"

Rosie took Arlen's hand in hers. Her fingernails dug into his palm. Suddenly she felt a strength, a joining the fight, which she had never felt before. She had feared this moment, yet part of her had waited for this moment. It was her time. Safety or not, weapons or not, she would confront the demon from her past.

She looked straight at *him*. "You stole my childhood. You terrorized me. I hated that you ever touched me. You violated me. You defiled my childhood. You took away my right to choose. You terrorized Danny too. You were never a brother to him. You are nothing but scum. I hate you…" She paused, quivering. "Get out of here. Now." Her voice was a shout. A shout that everyone heard.

Arlen felt her whole little body pressing into him. So strong, yet so fragile. He planted his feet, letting her slight frame lean deeply against his side.

So this was it. This was the secret he had missed. This was what had made her so aloof, so cautious, so icy around the guys who had come to the farm just to have fun and put in some hours of work for a good barbecue, beer and bonfire. This was the source. Any confusion Arlen had had before now melted away.

He felt himself coiling, ready to spring into an attack. A bolt of fury had rushed through him. How dare she yell at him? She was a woman. No, just a girl. No, a woman. She had accused him. Rage flashed through him. He sought retaliation. He had wanted to shoot her, smash her face and throw her down.

But her words stunned him. She was right. He had been rotten. He would never admit any details to anyone, but the anger toward her evaporated and he felt a deep piercing shame. He recalled her parents. They had always been decent to him, maybe even loving. Something he never got from his own parents. Filling up within him, right next to his rage, was the sense that he did not want to dishonor their memory. To harm her would be a desecration of that memory. He motioned for the others to point their weapons down. Finally, he mumbled, "I'm sorry about your mom and dad."

Arlen picked up on the tone. There was not going to be a fight, not from this one. "Gentlemen, it's time for you to go." He continued to stand by her side, her fingers digging into his palms, and he looked each of them in the eye.

They turned, almost in unison, and walked away down the road.

There was no argument, no violence. The trespassers turned and left the way they came. Arlen and Rosie stood, watching them, until they disappeared from sight.

Then Rosie's knees buckled, and she slumped to the ground. She began to cry, then to sob, and Arlen sat down and gathered her silently into his arms. She cried and cried, racked with sobs, shaking violently. He continued to hold her until the sobs subsided, offering a shirtsleeve, a bandana, and then a jacket to dry her eyes. Even then they just sat there, on the hard, uneven ground, until the evening sun slanted its rays through the huge distant pines on the receding hills.

Chapter 15

November was colder than predicted. Farmers' Market had closed for the season. Rosie and Sam cleaned out the field, sold all their produce, and still had the chickens. What they did not have was a plan. They needed to buy feed for the chickens, and they needed to find new markets for the eggs.

Their plan had been to repair everything over the winter, do artsy-craftsy stuff during the long nights, and restore the greenhouse for March plantings, until the warm weather crops could be laid in. So they were both doing it. They were making a go of it; they were proving that this homestead, this sustainable farm, could work. But Sam seemed to find more reasons than Rosie to go to town to buy a drill bit, re-supply feed for the chickens, or repair some tool. Then he'd call to say he couldn't get back that night. Rosie wound up alone, with evening and morning chores.

In mid-November, a blizzard hit. The weekend before Thanksgiving, out of the west, the heavens poured forth a foot of snow. They couldn't drive. The huge drifts on the north side of the mountains quashed any hope of taking the truck to town for Thanksgiving. They spent hours each day chopping wood for the stove.

Sam finally broke it to her over breakfast, the morning after the snowstorm. "Ya know, Rosie, I've been thinking. We made out pretty well this past summer, but with the blizzard, we can't get into town until the snow melts."

"We'll have to think of other ways to make some money, Sam," said Rosie, flipping through a catalogue of herbal remedies. "You know, a lot of the stuff in these remedies grows wild here on the farm, and in the woods–"

"The thing is, Rosie, it's just not going like I planned," Sam interrupted. "I thought we'd be closer to town. I thought more folks would be out here. I thought…" He stopped. "The thing is, Tony and me, we've been talking. He and a friend and I can go in on a farm out in Chino Valley, closer to the highway, easier to get stuff to market. More of a real farming community. It's so isolated here."

"You're going to bail on me, is that it?" Rosie's neck and cheeks flushed with anger and surprise. She'd been working her butt off, and he was planning to ditch the whole project. Well, it wasn't a piece of cake for her either, but she was committed.

Sam hemmed. "Well, it hasn't been a piece of cake for either of us, and I'm not planning to be a farmer without a woman by my side. And …"

"And we're sure as heck not made for each other," Rosie retorted.

Sam tried to find righteous ground. "No, and you don't make it any easier. You get off on your attitude and–"

"Stop it right there, Sam," Rosie declared frostily. "I didn't plan for this to be the way it went either. I'm going to take a break."

She grabbed her coat, stuffed her wool-stockinged feet into knee-high snow boots, and stormed out, slamming the door, leaving Brutus and Bella still huddled by the fire.

She picked her way through fresh snow and aimed downstream under the apple trees. The cloudy steel creek roiled as a torrent from the storm rushed past. She stood on a large boulder and looked across to the field, where the irrigation PVC carved a smooth horizontal white-on-white outline against the snow. Tufts of pale sere grass poked through drifts.

What was this all about? She had been so sure that the farm would be a success. They had it all worked out. Then Tony and Arielle had dropped out, and she and Sam were left carrying the load. But they had pulled it off. They had proved it could be done. And, with another season, they'd even turn a profit. Maybe. Just the sheer labor of it had been far more exhausting than she had imagined. The long hours had been grueling. The fall was in fact a respite, because the fields were dead for the winter. Rosie watched the rushing dark water. What was their goal? Did the farm really matter? Apparently it didn't matter so much to Sam, because he was planning to bail. And he hadn't included her in his plans.

But then, she hardly included him either. It was Arlen who understood her dreams of a retreat center. And maybe farming wasn't her ultimate life choice. It had been far more exhausting than she'd imagined. Nights, she was too tired for anything but sleep. And, at times like right now, when the only person within ten miles was a guy she couldn't even talk to, the farm was isolated.

If he went with Tony, who would take care of the chickens? Could she stay in the mountains alone? Had she come to forge a life as a farmer, or just to escape the past? And was the past still really haunting her? Or was she ready to look at something else? After all, *he* had, of all people, actually appeared last month. Thank God Arlen had come for the weekend. It wasn't the guns that made her feel safe, it was knowing that Arlen could talk anyone down. And she had found her voice and stood up to *him*. Something she had never thought could happen. Something she had feared and wanted. And he had left, shamed. So what next?

"I'm not ready for this," she cried to herself, her vision blurring.

Suddenly, Rosie heard a double *crack-crack* of a rifle, then the tan body of a mountain lion fell past her, crashing into the creek. Startled, she slipped and heard another *crack*, this time her shin, as she, too, careened against the sharp rocks.

After a heavy *thud*, Rosie lost consciousness.

"Oh, my God!" Sam held onto the .30-30 as he grabbed his boots and floundered through the snow toward her. He had come onto the porch to rationalize, to explain, to justify, when he saw the big cat crouched on a huge boulder just behind her, ready to spring. In a flash he had the rifle and took aim. Two shots in rapid succession found their mark. So the cat didn't get its prey.

He reached the creek to see her legs in awkward disarray. The left leg was bent in the wrong direction. He felt around and found a lump on the back of her head. Probably a concussion. She was breathing but unconscious.

In all their talks about the big "What If," Sam had never imagined that he'd actually have to shoot a mountain lion. Worse yet, he never imagined that either of them would be badly injured. He rushed back to the house and grabbed his cell phone.

"Benny, Benny, you gotta help me. Rosie's been hurt, and I can't drive her out. The snow's blocking the road," Sam shouted into the phone, as if that would bring help faster.

"Hold on, take it easy." Benny, now a licensed Emergency Medical Technician at Yavapai Regional Medical Center in Prescott, was trying to piece it together. "Slow down and tell me what happened. I need to know so we can figure out what to do next."

Sam recounted the situation as best he could.

"We'll need to get Air-Evac from Yavapai Regional to fly out and pick her up. Sam, I need you to help me out. Can you start as big a bonfire going as you can in the field or driveway, so we can see you as we fly in? And Sam, you know we can't land the chopper. We'll have to stay in a high hover. We'll have to count on you to put her into the body harness so we can hoist her up. It'll be sturdy but flexible. So be really careful with her neck. You don't know what damage there is."

Sam wedged a sheet of plywood under Rosie from her head to her hips. He slid her out of the creek, cut off all the wet clothes, and wrapped her as best he could in a huge, dry down quilt. He started a bonfire in the drive, keeping the dogs inside.

The next half hour was the longest of his life. Finally, the *whup-whup-whup* of the rotors honed in on the farm. The pilot came to a high hover, so that the blades wouldn't hit any trees or catch an edge in the hillside. Sam and Benny used hand signals, since they couldn't hear above the noise. Benny crouched at the opening and lowered a body harness. Sam slipped Rosie into it, feet first, then the hips, slowly, then the head and shoulders.

He brushed her hair lightly. "You'll be okay, girl, I know it. I just know it."

He waved for them to lift her up. The pilot pushed the cyclic forward, the rotor disk tilted forward, pulling the fuselage forward. The copter curled up and over the tree line, swung back to the northeast, rose again, and soon disappeared over the trees.

The cat lay dead in the creek. It was lithe, muscular. The bullets had left clean holes, but blood gushed into the water. Sam's emotions warred over the loss of such a rare, wild beauty. Despite his posturing, he wasn't a hunter. But there hadn't been a choice. It was the cat or Rosie. He'd made an instantaneous decision, and his instincts were right. He hauled the animal in a wet tarp up the slope to the drive. With a huge burst of energy, he threw it over the side into the bed of the truck and packed it in tight with snow and straw.

Benny greeted Danny and Arlen in the waiting room of the ICU at the Medical Center. "She's unconscious. I think the doctor will be out soon." They sat down. "Sam lifted her safely into the sling. She has a broken leg. Concussion too. But no spinal cord damage."

So began the waiting. They took turns entering the room to seek an indication that she might be waking. Finally, Rosie became aware of her surroundings. Veils of memory loss dropped away. First, she recognized Danny, then Benny, then Arlen. Sam was able to drive to town the next day. He explained what had happened.

"A mountain lion? Really? Well, you finally felled some big game. Glad you had that AK-47 with you after all."

Rosie tried to joke with him, since part of her recalling the day of her fall was the reminder that he had quit and was leaving the farm.

"Actually, the .30-30 did the job. I never needed an AK-47, Sam admitted. "But I would have picked different circumstances," he added, regretting their argument. Regretting that the argument had led to her near-fatal accident, had led to him killing the cat to save her life. "But I took him to a taxidermist. Maybe he should go on the wall across from the fireplace at the farm."

"Sam, I think you earned it," Danny said. "If it hadn't been for your quick thinking, Rosie would literally be dead meat. And then you called for Air-Evac and got her ready to go. Rosie and I have a lot to thank you for."

"Except that I'm pulling out of the farm. I'm not such a good friend after all."

Danny tried to smooth things over. "Well, the timing's good in one sense. Rosie can't go back there now. So it's good you're not stuck all alone out there."

"I'll be back," Rosie interrupted, attempting to be fully alert. "Just give me a few weeks of therapy. I have other plans for the farm…"

Her head fell back on the pillow in exhaustion. She raised her head again. "Brutus and Bella?"

"They're with Willie and me in Flag," answered Danny. "Those three are having a grand old reunion."

Arlen rubbed the exposed toes outside her cast with his rough, warm hands. "Let's just take it one step at a time, okay? Doesn't all have to be solved." He poured out some lotion, warmed it in his hands, and continued to rub the toes from the broken leg, then the other foot. "I'd think the next plan is, what about physical therapy after the hospital? You took a bad spill. There's the broken leg, but there's also the shock to your spine, hip and shoulder. And the concussion. You may even have some scrambled thoughts for a while. You'll need at least a few weeks. Could be months."

Rosie had to admit he was right. But she hated to. She had been trying so hard to be the one who called the shots, made the decisions, was right on target. The injury and this whole split with Sam had thrown a wrench into her plans. Not only that. She felt such overwhelming gratitude to Sam, for killing the cat and calling Benny; to Benny, for being part of the Air-Evac; to Danny, for all his caring; and to Arlen, for his calm in the crises with Dubya and with *him*. And for being here to break everything into smaller pieces. Bite-size pieces she could understand. She realized that both her thoughts and emotions were scrambled.

She didn't want to admit that she needed a lot of help.

Chapter 16

Despite attempts from Danny and Arlen to keep her away, Rosie returned to the farm in mid-January. The early snow of November had melted. It was all but empty. Sam had relocated the chickens, resettling on a farm in Chino Valley with some friends of Tony. The coop was barren and lifeless. Temperatures had dropped again. Hard, irregular cakes of dirt and parched clumps of love grass mottled the field. Clear Creek ran hard and fast, dirty and slate-gray from the earlier snowmelt.

The only sign of life came from Brutus and Bella, who were happy to return to the freedom of the farm after taking turns with Danny and Arlen while she recuperated. Arlen had let her and the dogs stay at his house, with no strings attached, while she worked intensely with one of the best physical therapists in the state. She had reluctantly agreed with Danny that she would stay in Phoenix or Flagstaff until the cast came off and therapy was complete.

But it was now January, and despite the guys' logic, Rosie returned. She knew Sam had moved, but there was something at the farm she needed to understand. She wasn't sure what it was. But it was there, out in the forest, that she felt she would find some answers.

The farm was still and silent. The absence of so much activity, so suddenly, was like a drop in the wind after being at full sail in the middle of the lake. There she was, without so much as a gust, not knowing exactly what it even meant to "come back."

What was it she was thinking of when she drove the Jeep and her canines back up the hill? Another season of farming? Life as a hermit? What about mountain lions? Bears? Now, at least, she would not step outside without her .38 or a rifle in hand. She was sure *he* was gone for good. Brutus and Bella guaranteed an early-warning system. No, she didn't fear for her safety. But she had invested so much in being here. She had to stay and find out what was meant for her, what to do, who to be?

Early in the afternoon, while the southern sun still gave some light to the meadow, Rosie donned boots and parka. A thin sheet of unbroken snow covered the path to her parents' clearing among the pines and junipers. She sat upon a flat rock at the end of an old stone wall, a few yards from the spot where she and Danny had dispersed their commingled cremains. She sat for a long time, until a chill set in.

Heavy snow clouds crowded the sky. The temperature plunged. She hauled a large store of firewood onto the veranda and set a fire in the fireplace. She inspected the house as Sam had left it. Messy. There would be days of cleaning, sorting, deciding where things belonged, what to keep, what to toss.

Upstairs in the loft the herbs she had harvested over the summer — spearmint, cliff rose, hollyhock, mullein, and shepherd's purse — had dried. A wealth of teas and tinctures awaited her creative touch.

After dinner, Rosie stoked the fire high, brought extra logs in for the night, and settled into a huge armchair with a quilt and a thick writing pad. She wrote to her parents, first the angry letter she had been afraid to admit, the one she knew that she needed to write.

"Mom and Dad:

"I don't know where to begin. Now that you're gone for good, I can't tell you what I never had the guts to say before.

"I'm so angry! I felt betrayed all those years that you let him stay in the house, in our family. Couldn't you tell that he abused me and Danny? He was mean, he was sneaky, and we were terrified."

She wrote page after page, detailing the abuse and her pervasive feeling of fear, a fear she had to mask for fear he'd do something worse — describing the deep feeling of abandonment and desolation that her parents, the two people she should have been able to count on the most, did not protect her.

Eventually she had said it all. She rose, let the dogs out briefly, paired a slow-burning oak log with a large fast-burning pine, and re-kindled the fire. Back in the armchair, she let a sip of red wine linger on her tongue. Something had finally gone out of her.

She picked up the pen and began again. *"Dear Mom and Dad..."*

This time she wrote a letter of loss and longing. About the good things she remembered from her childhood — the ballet classes, the swim meets, trips to the farm, tossing pebbles in the creek, occasional glimpses of deer and javelina. Being held in Mom's arms when she scraped her knee. Dad teaching her how to fire the .22. Bird watching with Mom. Starting the pump with Dad. Making s'mores around the fire pit while Danny played guitar.

After a long time, Rosie realized that this letter would never be complete. She knew, too, that it would never be delivered. She signed it, "I love you, Rosie." Then she slept.

Around midnight, soft as a kitten, snow started falling. Had she been awake, she would have seen the first delicate swirls of white against the darkness. After several hours, the winds picked up and by morning there were drifts in the driveway up to the windows of the Jeep. Yet, all in all, it was not a deep snow, just buffeted about wildly.

The entire farm was a pure, all-encompassing white. Only the bare branches of the apple trees, and the dark evergreens, stood out in contrast. The thermometer hovered around 31 degrees.

The cord of firewood, stacked close against the porch wall, stayed dry. The cold and cloudy weather intensified. Rosie stayed indoors, stoking the fires in both the stove and fireplace.

At first, she read the books that had accumulated over the years — a book on trees in the Southwest, some Zane Grey novels, and the books she had read as a child–*Ten Apples Up on Top, Cat in the Hat*, and *The Secret Garden*. Thoughts surfaced and entered her journal — overcoming fear, living with pain, summer's dirt-filled profusion versus winter's stark purity.

Thoughts emerged about everyone who had visited the farm, from Arielle with her melodic voice to pony-tailed Professor Pete. She thought of Benny, how quiet but thoughtful he had been, a major force in the airlift. Arlen wove in and out of her consciousness, his disarming humor and ability to defuse situations. And *him*–he seemed so insignificant now. For a split second, seeing him with his friends, all loaded with pistols or rifles, the terror had returned. But she had found her voice. Arlen had made a quiet but clear statement. They had gone. Her nightmare re-appeared once since that day, pale and receding into the distance. After that, it did not return.

It snowed again. Rosie read about teas and tisanes – the herbal mixtures she could concoct from nearby plants. The mint was refreshing. The chamomile relaxed before sleep. Another would aid digestion. She made up a few batches and experimented to see if the touted qualities could be felt for real. One afternoon she mixed the fragrant fragments of the tea leaves for relaxation and for sleep, and she fell into a doze in front of the fireplace, the dogs resting on the floor by the couch.

The first *tap-tap-tap* was too soft for the human ear. But soon the taps were a little louder. In the window next to the front door Rosie saw the faces of three women, bundled up against the snow, each with gray hair framing youthful faces.

"May we come in? We heard about your farm. We heard you were here, and we wanted to share some time," said the one with the pinkest cheeks, as they made themselves at home and hung wet gloves on the screen in front of the fire.

After a few sniffs, Brutus's and Bella's tails wagged and the visitors became invited friends.

"What are your names? How did you hear about the farm?" Rosie brought tea from the stove.

"I'm Terry, and these are my sisters, Polly and Mel," answered the one who seemed most slender after the parkas were shed. "We brought some things in our packs and hope to pass the time with you for a day or two, if that's okay, before returning to the 'real world.' We brought food. I see you have a guitar. Maybe you would enjoy some music with us?"

"I'd love some music," Rosie answered. "I've really missed not having someone to sing with, to harmonize with, since my friend decided not be part of the farm with me."

"I'm the one with the most songs," Polly said. "If we sing in the proper spirit, our chorus will become like sacred poetry. Terry actually brings to us the power of dance, which she can make holy when you and I play and sing together."

"What does Mel do, then?" Rosie asked. It seemed that each one had a special talent.

Mel gave a quirky smile: "I expose tragedy. When there has been a sad or traumatic event, I can help dramatize the elements needed to lift this burden from our hearts."

They had dinner first. A large pot of curried lentils warmed on the stove, and the sisters had brought fresh greens for a salad and a loaf of *paisano* bread. The sustenance warmed them and prepared them for the evening. They began with silence, gathered close by the hearth, sharing red wine.

Rosie tuned her guitar. Mel took Daniel's hand drum from the corner and accompanied Rosie. Polly sang soprano.

Polly knew every song Rosie suggested. Terry slipped into a skirt and began to dance. Polly's songs were plaintive at first, and Terry was seemingly unsure. But Mel kept a steady rhythm. Terry's bare feet began to thump and glide with confidence. She invited Rosie to join her. Rosie picked her African skirt from a drawer, wrapped it around her, slipped off her shoes, and joined hands with Terry.

The songs moved into anger. Mel kept tapping a haunting rhythm on the drums. Rosie was surprised at first, but her feminine rage found its center and Terry's heels thumped fiercely on the wood floor. It was if Terry knew. Rosie pounded her rage into the floor and held Terry's hands as a lifeline. The fire and the dance brought a sweaty glow to their faces. Time was suspended in a space of united feelings.

After awhile, the music resolved into more melodic lyrics, as if preparing them to return to the present. Their chorus, rich with harmony, rose above the mundane. They sang songs of love, songs of sadness, songs of loss, and, finally, songs of peace. Quietly, the sisters unrolled their sleeping bags and slept on the floor with the dogs nearby. Rosie slept under the down quilt on the couch, right in front of the hearth.

They stayed for two days and two nights. There was food enough and the meals were easy. The first day they stayed indoors. Polly and Mel took to cleaning out dirty cabinets, and Terry helped rearrange the bookshelves. They cleaned windowpanes. The place sparkled for the first time in Rosie's memory.

The second day they asked Rosie to take them somewhere special. She led them out the back door up the hill. In parkas and snow boots, they gracefully ascended, winding back and forth, finally arriving at a small shelter.

"This is my Yoga House," Rosie said, inviting them inside. Each woman stood in a corner of the room, facing the others. They invited Rosie to lead them in some asanas, some physical postures that would guide them into meditation. Rosie began with a pose of arms outreached, palms up, an invitation to a time of sharing. Mel encouraged her softly. "Do not shy away from what is painful: in bringing our focus in meditation upon this place we can bring it to the full light of day. We can sweep away the dust and cobwebs of darkness. We can transform tragedy into something beautiful."

Rosie modeled a forward bend. They stretched their backs and legs. Dropping to the floor, she brought up her chest as if to face her past. With arms fully stretched, she came to a kneeling position. The sisters did likewise. Then they rose to a standing position, to the asana of a warrior, focusing on the physical balance and the meditative discipline to gain inner strength in order to know who each of them really might be.

Again raising her arms to the sky, bring them down in a wide circle, and placing her hands on her heart, Rosie paused in thanks. She then put her hands above her head again and moved into the asana of a complete back bend, opening her body and spirit to the challenges of her truths that she must confront.

After returning to upright and performing a few more balancing stretches, Rosie motioned the sisters to join her in the resting posture, or Savasana. Breathing deeply, she entered dhyana, meditation, on who she really was.

Finally, they rose slowly to a comfortable sitting position. They held this pose silently for several long, peaceful moments. Then, together, they greeted each other: "Namaste."

That evening they played, sang, danced, and called upon the spirits of the universe to be with them, to lift their sorrows, to embrace their strengths and weaknesses, and to celebrate their beauties.

Just as they were about to retire, Mel discovered the tablet with Rosie's letters. "What's this? 'Mom and Dad'?"

Rosie hesitated. She'd forgotten them, and now it was embarrassing to have others see what she'd done.

"Oh, nothing."

Mel reached over and touched her hand. "Rosie, remember how I said I can sometimes move people to a different space? Now may be the time for you, or your Mom and Dad, to move from tragedy to a better space. Tell me."

So Rosie told them about her parents, her childhood, the letter of rage, and the letter of love.

Mel handed her the pad. "Would you like to be able to be with your parents, to let them know how you feel? Not physically, but in your heart, in the heart that *knows?*"

"Yes. Yes, if…"

"Take the letter of anger first. Put it in the fire, one page at a time, and as you drop each page into the flames, ask your parents to hear you."

One by one, Rosie dropped each leaf of the letter on top of the logs, watching the paper curl, darken, and disappear as the flames burst higher. She closed her eyes. Mom and Dad appeared before her, sadness in their eyes. "We hear you, honey. We are so immeasurably sorry."

After a time, Mel handed her the other letter. "Do you want to burn this one too?"

"If I save it, will I be able to see them later?"

"When you find the right time to share it with them, come to this fireplace. Tuck it away now. You'll know when it is time and what you should do. They will be here with you. I think you know, already, that they will always love you."

"Yes." It was simple. It was true.

At breakfast on the third morning, Rosie mustered the courage to ask what had been in her mind during the whole visit. "I sometimes feel you aren't giving me the whole story," she began. "I feel as if someone sent you, but I can't think of anyone I know who would think of sending just such perfect guests as the three of you."

"It may be a clue if we tell you what our parents named us," Mel began. "My birth name is Melpomene, but I couldn't go around town with that, so Mom called me Mel for short."

"And I am Polyhymnia, but, same thing, Dad called me Polly for short."

And Terry, "My given name was Terpsichore, but, again, who in the real world could even pronounce that? So I prefer Terry."

Rosie was puzzled. "Those are big names, ladies–I want to call you my sisters–but I still don't quite get what's been happening here."

"Well," Mel took Rosie's hands in hers across the breakfast table, "let's just say we were just the visit you needed."

Polly gathered the sisters' belongings together. "It was a wonderful visit, Rosie, and if you don't mind, I will always consider you my sister."

Rosie found herself welling up with emotion, for the sisters she never had, for the parents she had lost, for the one who had terrorized her childhood, for her gratitude at having Danny as such a gentle brother, and for the people who had been good to her at the farm.

"Thank you so much for coming." She bundled all three into a group hug. "Will I ever see you again? Do you live in Phoenix, or Flagstaff, or Prescott? Where can I find you?"

Terry sat down and pulled on her boots. "You may find us, or maybe not. If you drive east on the Carefree Highway, there is a Healing Center — physical therapy, music therapy, counseling. But if you don't find us exactly," and she looked around at Mel and Polly, "I think you'll find us in your heart easily enough. You might even become one of us."

They left with more embraces and smiles, patting the dogs, and then trekked quietly, side by side, out the drive and down the road.

Rosie poured another cup of tea. She piled the fire high, put a screen in front of the flames, and fell on the couch into a deep slumber.

Benny had succeeded in driving in through the melting snow. He lived in Prescott now, and had landed a full-time job as an EMT tech with Yavapai Regional Medical Center. But he had hitched a ride to Tuba City, to ask his sister Margaret and his aunt Charlotte to come with him on this visit to Rosie. Male relatives, too, had victimized Margaret — more than once. Benny invited Charlotte to be with them because she had been witness to the sacred dances and had participated in many of the women's sweat lodge cleansing ceremonies.

Charlotte was considered an elder in the tribe, a wise woman, despite being only in her forties. She would bring insight and wisdom that Benny and his sister were yet to gain.

They found the snow fresh, untouched, light. The drive was easier than expected. Together they waited in the driveway, considering whether to knock on the door. Normally, since Benny had been here before with his Anglo friends from Prescott, he might have knocked, and he knew the dogs would remember him.

This time, however, was different. To wait until acknowledged was the way of the *Dine*, the Navajo way. To show respect for the person you came to visit. He was here on some business for his people. His sister and auntie were here with him. And so, they would greet his friend Rosie in the Navajo way.

The fire had burned to embers in the late morning by the time Bella started wagging her tail anxiously at the door. Brutus joined her, and then in unison they began to whimper and whine, meaning, "We need out, please."

Rosie got up and opened the door. Benny was sitting quietly in his truck. Two women were with him.

"Benny, what are you doing here? Who…?" Rosie walked stiffly to the edge of the porch. The leg that had broken still ached from the cold. "Come on in, don't just sit there in your truck." The dogs wanted to stay out and play for a bit, so she ushered her guests inside. "Tea?" Not waiting for an answer, she brought them tea of dried spearmint leaves from the creek that had been steeping in the pot. They sat by the hearth.

"Rosie, I want you to meet my sister, Margaret, and my aunt Charlotte." They all shook hands, murmured polite greetings, and sipped quietly. A silence, not of the Anglo style but completely comfortable and centered, grew upon them. Finally Benny broke the silence.

"You're a lot better. Glad to see it. You were pretty much a mess when we brought you in to Yavapai Regional. Wow! I never expected to see that much action back in November, when I was first on the job."

"I was lucky too, to have you guys on it so fast. Must hand it to Sam — he packed me into the sling for the helicopter pretty well, though I don't remember any of it. I guess if he'd done a bad job I might not be walking today. Or thinking either." She cupped her hands around the mug and let the steam rise. The faint aroma of local spearmint wafted warmly under her nose.

"Wait! I just realized. Did you drive in? I thought the snow was too deep to drive, so I was just going to wait for a week or so." She then remembered her visitors, as if muses in a dream. "Benny, you wouldn't believe. I had the most unusual visit from three women. They just left this morning …"

"No, we didn't see anyone. And as we drove in, the road had not been traveled. No tire tracks, no footprints. Completely fresh.".

"But?"

He didn't seem to have any idea of what she was talking about. She looked out the window. She did not see footprints leaving in the drive. But she was sure the sisters had visited. Their presence was a vivid memory.

In any event, Benny was here, and he had brought two members of his family.

"What brings you here on this snowy journey? Did you come all the way from Tuba City?"

Charlotte spoke first. "Rosie, my nephew Benny has told us about you. About your suffering." She paused. "My niece Margaret, Benny's sister, has suffered as you have. It is a terrible thing for a young woman to be violated."

Benny was patting the dogs, allowing the women to direct the conversation. Yet he was very present.

In the mystical space of the spirit, Rosie realized that they understood about her past. About the violation, the terror, the self-loathing, the inability to control life. The way Benny had held his space and silence after the nightmare, the lightning speed with which he tackled and subdued Jack – these were borne of intuitive understanding and a desire to honor and protect.

She then understood about the sweat lodge, why he had

asked her if she was ready, why he had described the sweat as something spiritual as well as physical. And why, until now, he had not returned to help her finish the lodge.

Moments of silence defined their conversation. It was of sacred import that humans should not interfere with the power of the Great Spirit in working its healing truth among them. Finally Benny joined back in.

"Margaret, Aunt Charlotte and I – we would like to invite you to a sweat ceremony today. Here at the farm. We brought some tarps and a sacred blanket to cover the frame. We'll need to start a fire in the outside fire pit, heat the rocks, and then place them inside. But the main part of this ceremony is you.

"The sweat is very powerful. It can release toxins from your body. It can purify your spirit.

"Rosie, you have suffered many shocks to your body and to your soul. Margaret and Charlotte want to join you in a sweat to help in a purification ceremony. This summer I said it would happen when you were ready. Do you feel now that you can be ready?"

"Yes, I think so. Some things have happened since you were here last. Did you hear?"

"I know someone was here. Someone you had to confront."

"Benny, I'm beginning to want to let go of what haunts me. To move forward. Does this mean I'm ready?"

Charlotte laid a smooth brown hand, laden with silver and turquoise rings, gently upon Rosie's knee.

"Yes, Rosie, this means you are ready."

Since the snowstorm had soaked all the wood on the ground, they carried firewood from under the porch across the creek and started a fire. After it gained strength, Benny hauled softball-sized rocks, the roundest he could find, and laid them in the fire. He examined each one to be sure they would not explode from the heat. Fortunately, the well-known Bradshaw granite lay everywhere. He gathered a full supply. The moisture of the rocks sizzled in the fire, but they kept adding dry logs and after awhile there was a good pile of rocks for the sweat.

Margaret helped Rosie dig a pit under the frame for the hot rocks inside the frame. Then the three women laid several tarps across the dome, saving the blanket for last, near the opening. They secured the covers with twine so that little or no light or moisture could enter the hut, or escape.

Charlotte and Margaret took Rosie back to the house. While they were in the bedroom, Benny took Danny's hand drum in the living room and found a place outside by the fire pit. He sat on a large tree stump and quietly tapped his fingers, sometimes the butt of his palm, on the skin. The soft steady rhythm vibrated lightly within the house.

Since there was a man present, they would cover their bodies. At Charlotte's direction, they removed all their clothing and jewelry. Then each one donned a towel around her middle, hitched above the breast. Lastly, against the cold, they put on their boots and parkas and returned.

Benny took a large shovel and carried over a dozen heated rocks through the low opening. He placed them close together in the dirt pit dug by Margaret and Rosie. Then he hauled two five-gallon buckets of water over one hundred feet from the creek to the door of the hut. Charlotte had found some smaller containers and a dipper. She poured water from one of the big buckets into them. Margaret and Rosie each took one of the smaller buckets and placed them inside the opening, along with the dipper. Then the women, shedding their parkas, crawled through the low opening into the darkness, the only light coming from the red-hot coals of the rock-bed.

"Benny's not part of this?" Rosie asked as they moved inside.

"This one will be just a woman's experience," Charlotte explained. "Sweats are generally same-sex only." Margaret nodded. She had only been to one sweat before. It had been a sweat to help her cleanse from her past and purge the evil done to her. The ceremony was easier with only female participants.

"But Benny is very much a part of this ceremony," Charlotte added. "You'll hear him. He will be drumming and probably chanting traditional songs. You know, Rosie, you mean a lot to him. He will be with us, just outside."

It was dark inside. Each of the women found room around the pit to sit, cross-legged, touching Mother Earth, facing each other. They formed a small triangular circle. At first, it was oppressively hot. Charlotte poured water on the rocks and steam billowed out, trapped in a small space, surrounding the three women. The steam, rising from the rocks, thickened the air. Rosie found it hard to breathe.

Charlotte began to speak, softly. First she recognized the direction of the East, of daybreak, birth, new beginnings — the awakening after a long sleep of death of the soul, of sorrow. "We ask of the morning star of the east that we may gain wisdom that will follow us in all our endeavors."

Next, Charlotte addressed the South, the color of white, for peace, asking for growth and healing.

Margaret and Rosie followed Charlotte's face and words intently. They were silent. Charlotte invoked the West, asking for a spirit guide for the participants. "The West can be seen as black, or death. We look into the face of that which had dealt a death blow to our body or spirit and we ask for guidance to understand and face our disease."

Margaret began to moan softly, a long low wail in Navajo that was barely audible. Rosie focused on her breathing. As the steam and heat intensified, she felt as though she was accompanying Margaret into a very dark place. They shared time in the silence.

After awhile Margaret spoke in English. "I was violated by my uncle and by my older male cousin," she said to the Spirit. "I felt that I would die, that I should die." She breathed, moaned again, sighed. Finally Margaret appeared to be released from a bondage that had held her close to a place of death.

Again they sat in the dark silence. Again Margaret spoke. "Give me the courage to tell my family the truth, and if they do not believe me, to endure and become clean through my honesty."

Rosie felt herself delving into emotions that she had long suppressed. She found herself uttering, "Help me be strong. Give me courage. Help me overcome the shame, the anger."

The flap opened and Benny's long shovel added two more hot stones. The flap closed, returning them to darkness. Charlotte ladled more water on the red centers. Steam burst forth toward them.

The women remained silent again for some time. Rosie could hear the quiet breathing of each one – in, out, in, out. Rosie was sweating profusely. The waters of life, her waters of life, were pouring out of every pore, mixing with the water from the stream, the waters of life coming from the earth, the steam made by the rocks. In this hot darkness occurred a mingling of the waters of all life coming from Mother Earth and returning.

Rosie could not tell how long they remained thus. Suddenly, after period of discomfort and inner rumbling, she felt a release, a pouring out from her body, of something dreaded and old. She exhaled sharply, as if she had been holding her breath for a very long time. Lightness entered her being. The two other women watched her in silence, honoring her experience. After awhile, Rosie could feel herself returning to a sense of normalcy, but one that was completely different from all her life before. Something deep and terrible had been released from her, something that had trapped her all these years. She was no longer living in a cage. Her spirit had been cleansed. She would be able to stand on her own, to walk in freedom and grace.

The final prayer was to the North, the color of Blue. Charlotte asked for courage, endurance, cleanliness and honesty. Rosie felt the two women taking her hands, holding them in an unbroken circle. Despite the heat, she felt strengthened and lifted as they held her, leading her away from death and sorrow, through endurance, toward wisdom.

Charlotte nodded. It was time to draw to a close. One by one they crawled out of the entryway into the bright afternoon, snow still everywhere on the ground. They slid into boots and parkas. Then they joined hands and walked a little distance away from Benny, close to the stone wall where a drift of snow had accumulated. There, one by one, each woman shed her parka and boots and towel. Rosie lay naked in the snow, letting the cleansing of the earth's snowy waters work on her soul and spirit. She felt as if she were experiencing a second birth, a rediscovery of her body, purified from abuse.

Silently they rose, wrapped themselves in their parkas and boots, and returned to Benny. Once inside the house, Rosie, Margaret and Charlotte changed into dry clothes and made the evening meal. Benny had walked up the path along the creek, alone with his own thoughts. The evening was quiet, with gentle conversation. No one tried to put into words what had happened in the sweat. For Rosie, the healing had begun.

She was being restored to harmony.

Chapter 17

The four rose before dawn. They would all leave together. Charlotte and Margaret had work to return to in Tuba City, over two hours north of Flagstaff.

As they walked to the trucks, they could hear a loud crack, then a scraping, and then a rippling crash. The top half of a Ponderosa pine, suspended in its trajectory for almost a year after breaking off in a winter wind, broke free from the juniper in which it had been suspended and pummeled the forest hillside.

Margaret turned, taken by surprise. "What was that?"

Rosie remembered her day with Danny, scattering the ashes of her parents among the trees above the meadow. "It is just the business of life and of loss, coming to its proper conclusion. A tree that had been broken, and was suspended for awhile, is now laid to rest."

Margaret rode in front with Rosie, the dogs in the back seat. Benny and Charlotte were in their truck. As normalcy resurfaced, Rosie felt there were many unanswered questions.

"Margaret, what was it about that whole process?"

Margaret looked ahead to the road, with a bittersweet smile. "It can't all be explained. And it is not a complete process. Memories of pain, of trauma, have come up for me since my first sweat, and they may for you too. I do not think of myself as cured, or healed. But I have begun to embrace the process. Honestly, Rosie, I think some of the reason we Dine are quiet so much of the time is because we simply understand that it's a mystery. We know of the power of the Great Spirit and of Mother Earth. We know of the healing, purifying power that happens in a sweat. But we can't say exactly why. But you know, it doesn't matter. Because it feels true, and right."

"What about Benny? Now that I have experienced the sweat, I can understand why it's mostly same-sex. But he was there, and he was participating in very traditional medicine. Up to now, knowing him through Prescott and his EMT training, I had thought he'd be only for modern medicine."

"My brother is a rare mix. He is determined to learn the modern medicine and bring it to our Nation. I may study nursing next year. I too want to help my people. When Benny's in Prescott, he studies modern medicine. Now he is training to gain invaluable EMT experience. But when he's visiting home, he studies with one of the elders the traditional medicine and ceremonial chants. He has a good heart. I know he feels guilty about what happened to me. But he couldn't have prevented it. He's been a good brother to me. Charlotte believes he will in time become one of a new generation of medicine men, more knowledgeable and wiser, enriching what is valuable in the old with what is valuable from the new."

In Flagstaff, they first let Brutus and Bella into Danny's house to rejoin Willie. Then they went to Danny's restaurant for breakfast. Danny joined them.

As they finished, Benny spoke carefully. "Danny, I'm glad we are friends. And your sister. I never imagined I would have a *bilagaana* sister. Rosie is that sister."

Margaret added, "I feel the same way, Rosie. I'm so glad we know each other. She handed Rosie a small package of tissue paper. "This is for you, Rosie. We did not have to fight off a bear in the forest, but we wrestled demons. I want you to have the bear with you, as your totem to give you strength."

Rosie opened the tissue slowly. Centered on a necklace of hand-hammered links was a silver-pendant in the shape of a bear. In the dark, unpolished arrow that ran from its mouth through its body, marking the breath of life, rested a tiny nugget of gold. Rosie fingered it carefully. "And the gold, the most precious of metals. As your friendship is to me," she said, as she fixed the clasp behind her neck.

They said their goodbyes, the women embracing each other. Rosie held Benny's hands in hers, for a silent moment, and let him go.

After they left, Daniel brought out a tattered 9"x12" envelope and handed it to Rosie. "This came to the house. It was addressed to both of us, but it's for you."

"What is it? It has the name of some law office on it. What've I done wrong?"

"Nothing. Read it." He took the papers out of the envelope and placed them side-by-side in front of her.

The first one was on legal letterhead. "We are sorry to inform you of the death of Alden Thoreau Wainwright, USMC Captain, in Flagstaff, on January 18."

While the three sisters were visiting, she thought.

"He has provided us with a copy of his will and life insurance policy from his status as a veteran. You are the sole beneficiary named in his life insurance policy."

Rosie looked up, stunned. "But Danny, we parted on such rotten terms. He almost killed Brutus. I never thought I'd hear from him again. Didn't want to."

"Read the letter, sis. It explains a lot."

The letter was shakily handwritten in pencil on lined paper, as if a few sheets had been purloined from the Kachina Convenience Mart where Hotchkiss worked.

"Dear Rosie,

"By now you may have forgotten everything about me except that I almost killed your beautiful Lab, Brutus. I don't think words can ever say how sorry I am, and how grateful that his wound has healed. Hotchkiss told me. I was glad that

young Navajo, Benny, knew instantly how to apply first aid. I was grateful for the fellow, Arlen, who took Brutus so quickly to a vet and provided a place for him to recover while you still ran the farm. I was grateful to Danny and Hotchkiss, for taking the gun away from me and getting me home to Flagstaff, where I could do you no further harm.

"And I was most grateful to you, my dear little Rosie, for bringing me to my consciousness. First, you reminded me of my beloved wife Jean, for whom I caused so much sorrow. Then, you showed me how lovely my daughter would have been, if I'd had a daughter.

"Third, and you may not remember this, you showed me, by your exquisite performance of dance to the African drum music on that cold December evening over a year ago, that we can safely transport ourselves away from the terrors that haunt us most.

"You may be able to tell from this letter that I am sober. As I said, you brought me to consciousness. I am so sad that Brutus had to be hurt in the process. But that moment — when I disgraced myself and all I had stood for in service to our country so many years ago, by misusing my powerful ability with a weapon, as a Marine — made me know I had to get sober. I knew I had to get counseling.

"It was hard. I first had to get to the VA in Phoenix. Hotchkiss drove me down. They had a terrific intake there–it's so much better than when I got out of the service in '72–and they hospitalized me immediately. I was in for both alcohol and PTSD — post-traumatic stress syndrome disorder — a pretty common "dual diagnosis" for returning vets from all the wars. If there's one thing I can thank Vietnam for, it's that diagnosis in the DSM IV–PTSD. It has started helping the VA treat folks like me who returned from combat an emotional wreck, but with no clue how to recover from their trauma.

"After the hospital, they had me on antidepressants and anti-anxiety drugs. More expensive than Smirnoff, but at least paid for by our loyal taxpayers – and there was no hangover. They referred me to a counseling center in Flagstaff, and I was doing pretty well there. I had some individual sessions

in a process called EMDR–something about rapid eye movement–helps you talk about the dark stuff without the waves of emotion that overwhelm you. And I participated in group sessions too, with fellow vets who knew what I'd been through. They understood.

"But, Rosie, I'd been a chain smoker for decades. It had caught up with me. By the time they diagnosed me with lung cancer, it was clear I was terminal. I chose to skip treatment and just try to make amends for all the shitty stuff I've done since I returned from 'Nam.

"It's New Year's Day. My main resolution is to leave you the best stuff I have. I've asked Hotchkiss and Danny to clean out my place, and they'll share all the ammo–you knew I had a reloading factory in my bedroom, didn't you? Hotchkiss will get the drums. Danny will get the guns. I think he'll sell the new ones and keep the museum pieces just for memorabilia.

"I had a little life insurance policy from the service. Not much, just $50,000. But I want you to have it. Maybe you can invest in a few yoga retreats. And I have a Navajo rug I'd like you to have. Maybe put it on a wall of the farmhouse.
"I'm getting hospice care at home now. I can see out my window that there's a new blanket of snow on the evergreens. There's a peace in the winter sky I haven't felt in years.

"Things are pretty much in order. I'm sober, I'm getting help. Some of the vets from the peer-counseling group come see me every day. They've promised they won't let me die alone.

"Thank you so very much for letting me see how beautiful my daughter would have been. I loved your spirit from the moment I saw you dance. I would have wondered about you always. If I hadn't been able to meet you at the farm it would have haunted me my whole life.

"Finally, I am so very, very sorry for the harm I did. Maybe the pain I caused Brutus can turn us all into more conscious, caring human beings.

"Yours affectionately,

"Alden Thoreau 'Dubya' Wainwright."

Rosie looked up at Danny. They held hands silently for a few moments across the table.

"I've gotta go back to work now, sis. Will you be there when I get home?"

"Not sure, bro. I have to tend to some unfinished business. Can you take care of the dogs for a few days? I'll let you know what's what."

As Rosie headed east on the Carefree Highway, toward Scottsdale, she spotted a low-slung adobe building on the north side of the road. Not one angle to it, just soft, solid curves. "The Muse Healing Center" read the discreet but clearly lettered sign in periwinkle blue against the buff-brushed marquee.

Smiling to herself, she made a mental note. She would soon return. She had work to do, she had a path to follow, and she was ready.

The same strings of big red hearts and cuddly bears from last year again adorned hardware, motors and checkouts. The store manager had hung them a month early in an attempt to lift spirits out of the winter doldrums.

Adriana was sipping a second cup of coffee from Ernesto's when she heard a flatbed cart grind across the spilled grains of sand and cement on the concrete floor. It headed toward motors. It carried something metal, square, solid. Dirty, old. Then she recognized the blue plaid flannel shirt and the dark curly hair of the young woman pushing the cart.

Arlen fiddled with a battery-run drill/driver on the shelf. It was almost a year since a young woman with mahogany curls and clear blue eyes had come into motors asking for his help. Last week he'd restocked motors with another Honda and a Briggs & Stratton, even though motors were slow this time of year. Just in case.

He had dropped ten pounds since Christmas and started pressing his jeans instead of just coming to work a little disheveled. Rosie'd been right about chorizo. More than that, he realized that he'd let himself go in a little personal pity party. He owed it to his better self to eat better, get in shape, and bring a little more professionalism to his job – and care to himself.

It was over a month since he'd let her and the dogs drive north, out of his life, back to a mountain farm that appeared to call to her like a siren. He'd finally had to let it go — let her go. He hadn't expected to, but he had given her his heart, not so much in words but in every quiet deed he could think of. It just seemed she was driven in another direction. He let out a long sigh of resignation. Another year.

"Excuse me, sir, can you help me? Seems I have this broken motor. I think I need a new one."

He knew the voice, the soft strong vibrancy.

"Rosie?"

A flatbed cart with a worn-out motor rattled toward him. The brown curls framed her face and the blue plaid shirt mirrored her eyes.

"You were right, Mr. Arlen. The old model won't work anymore. Took me awhile to realize it, but I do need a new motor. And I believe you're the man to help me."

He stood there, transfixed. She stepped around the flatbed with its dead motor, and handed him the motor's cord. It had frayed and fallen off.

She let her hand stay in his. She looked into his kind brown eyes. She recalled how she had first trusted him to invite him to the farm, almost a year ago. How she had been drawn to him, had felt safe. But how she'd been afraid to think of him as a man, as a man she could love, a man who might love her.

"I think I'm ready for a change."

"A new motor? That's a big investment, Miss Rosie." He picked up on her polite and gracious formality, as if at a dance. "Don't you want some time to consider?"

Lord, her eyes were just as beautiful as he remembered. And she was here. Here by her own choice.

"I've had some time to think it over. And...and I've learned a few things. I think it's time."

"It's almost noon," Arlen said. "Better to work out a deal on a full stomach. Wouldn't want to make such a decision in haste. Don't you agree? How about some lunch first?"

Her hand felt strong and soft in his. "I know of a whole foods restaurant nearby that just opened up. They have great salads. Want to give it a try?"

He looked a little trimmer than she remembered. Cutting back on chorizo? She gazed at the line of his body, from his warm brown eyes to the Arizona Flag buckle on his belt to the bottom of his fresh pressed jeans. His hands were still calloused and gently strong. Rosie looked back up at him, taking in the whole man, greeting what she saw with new-found trust.

She paused, caught her breath, and took a leap of faith.

"If you'll give it a try, so will I."

Questions for Discussion

1. What purpose did the African dance serve for Rosie?

2. How is it similar for Wainwright and drumming?

3. Why does Rosie decide to create an organic farm?

4. What does Arlen notice about Rosie? Does this attract him or not? Why?

5. At the farm, what values surface over mining? Guns? Property?

6. How does Benny fit in with, or not fit in, with the group from Prescott?

7. What does Rosie's dream signify? What does it bring up for you?

8. Why doesn't *he* have a name?

9. How does *he* rationalize what he did to Rosie? Have you ever experienced or known of similar rationalizations?

10. Why does Rosie decide to have Arlen take Brutus?

11. As Rosie's older brother, could or should Danny have done anything differently? Why or why not?

12. Did his decision not to fight Rosie and Arlen at the farm ring true? Could he have experienced remorse?

13. Who are the three visiting sisters?

14. What is the function of the sweat?

15. Do you know someone who has experienced trauma? Who do you or they see as a support group?

16. Several of the characters have been exposed to abuse and trauma. How do each of them begin to heal from their past? Is each path fitting for the individual person? What else might be useful in healing?

Contact the author at nanmar@cox.net

To purchase more copies, go to
rosiesgold.com or nancyhickmarshallbooks.org
Payment by Paypal

www.ingramcontent.com/pod-product-compliance
Lightning Source LLC
Chambersburg PA
CBHW072110170626
46813CB00004B/1497